My Life as a Dust Devil
by
Carly Berg

To the one I can always count on.

Copyright 2025 Carly Berg
Houston, Texas, USA
All rights reserved
Published by South Coast Books
Houston, TX
ISBN #979-8-9934878-2-3

Shocking hues of gold and orange splash across a periwinkle-tinted sky, in those magical moments before the sun drops behind the mountains.

Two women, one young, one middle-aged, open their back doors simultaneously and stride purposefully out onto their respective patios, which face each other across adjacent backyards.

They stand at attention and exchange curt nods, in accordance with established protocol. Then, in sync, each woman raises her right hand, middle finger extended, flipping the proverbial bird to the other.

Their task completed, they turn smartly and retreat back into their own homes. Thus ending another regular day in the suburbs of Roswell, New Mexico

.

To the nomad, change is home

"Mira! Look!" parrot-beak nose Maria José squawked, like it was the biggest thing to hit Roswell since the alien spaceship crash of 1947. Yep, Maria José Hernandez started it all, on her way back from sharpening her pencil. That girl sharpened her pencil more than anybody else in the whole school, her excuse to go around bothering her neighbors. If she wasn't the teacher's pet, she wouldn't have been allowed out of her seat in the first place. She wouldn't have seen my mother, Ree, doing her man-call dance.

My whole class got out of their seats without permission, in the middle of silent reading time. We crowded around the windows and gawked at Ree, who was dancing up on the bluffs. Ree swayed and twirled, her long hair swinging, a silhouette against the white-hot New Mexico sun. She was up so high that she looked miniature from here, a tiny dancing figurine like the plastic one that popped up whenever I opened the lid of the jewelry box Bonnie Sue had given me.

Our teacher, Mr. Villalobos, forgot to make us sit down. He came up behind us, watching too. He said, "agraciada" and "enviada por dios," half-whispering in awe as Ree danced. My Spanish was good enough to know what he said: "graceful," and "sent by god." I bet he wouldn't say that if he knew Ree was naked.

Thank god you couldn't tell that from here. Otherwise, I'd fall over right there, so mortified I'd die. I'd be all morted out then. Mortified. Mortally wounded. Then there'd be the mortician and the mortuary, see.

"What tribe?" some kid said, like it was a tribal dance or something. A rain dance would make sense, though. It was so dry out that me and Bonnie Sue had to use lip balm and artificial tears *and* sleep with humidifiers on our dressers, too. I snuck a look at Brynn, who knew me and my stepmom Bonnie Sue better than anybody else around here. Brynn's mom and Bonnie Sue were good friends. So Brynn would have heard plenty of chisme about Ree. Especially since Brynn clung to her mommy like a titty baby.

One time I even caught Brynn sitting on her mom's lap. I say I caught her, but Brynn didn't even have the snap to know she was supposed to be embarrassed. Nope, she just stayed right there where she was, a happy, happy titty baby. Brynn's face was as smooth and clueless now as it always was. For once, I was grateful that she was too babyish to understand anything. I chimed in with the others, "Yeah, what is that, a rain dance?"

White dust fluffed up in flurries in the distance outside, unsettled by an old pickup truck bouncing along the gravel road toward the bluffs, toward Ree. Rust-colored dirt puffs joined in when a cowboy also headed for the bluffs, galloping his horse across the dry scrubland. Dark smoke added to the multi-colored air pollution, exhaust from a motorcycle that sped along the paved road leading to the bluffs. Ree shattered the stillness and caused pollution, in the school and the desert beyond.

Why couldn't I have a normal mother like everybody else instead of a wild thing? I wanted a mother who would pick me up after school, with her clothes on. And who'd maybe even bake cookies for me and my friends once in a while. Or at least a mother who had a place I could go home *to*. Heck, I'd settle for a mother who I could call "mother" or "mom" instead of having to call by her first name. It's like Ree was letting me know right there not to expect much.

To be fair, my stepmom Bonnie Sue did all those nice mother things for me. But what Bonnie Sue didn't understand was you couldn't just fire your mother and get a new one any old time you found somebody who was better at the job. Nope. You were stuck with the mother you got, and she was stuck with you, whether either of you liked it or not.

Mr. Villalobos suddenly yelled at us to get back in our seats. He snapped the blinds shut on all four of the classroom windows, quick and sharp like he was mad. Had he noticed that Ree wasn't wearing any clothes? I bet he'd get in a ton of trouble for ooh-ing and ah-ing over a naked lady in front of us kids.

Even that massive mortification wasn't the end of it, though. Nope. Everybody just *had* to keep up the chisme about it for the rest of the day. It was like a nightmare in the middle of the day, a daymare.

In Science lab, the pretty teacher's aide, Miss Dell, said to Mr. Villalobos, "Did you see that lady dancing up on the bluffs? Wow, it was graceful. So inspiring. I about cried."

Mr. Villalobos raised his eyebrows. He pressed his lips together. *Dis-appro-val of the in-appro-priate.* Root: appro. The root wasn't always at the beginning of the word, see. I felt bad, like I had caused the silent clash between Mr. Villalobos and Miss Dell, and the uproar in the rest of the school, too. Well, I *did* always somehow seem to be at the center of the constant messes that popped up around me.

Later, it was my class's turn in the school library. I looked up "mort" and "appro" in the big Webster's dictionary, since it wasn't our class's day to use the computers. I heard old parrot-beak Hernandez in the next aisle of bookshelves. She was at it again. "What did you guys think of the bluff dancer?" Parrot-beak squawked her question to the two most popular girls in our class, who were also best friends with each other.

The cool girls' names were Selena and Madison but they usually called each other "bitch."

They were that hard, like teenagers already. Their pierced earrings looked super glam on them, too. They were the reason I got my ears pierced.

Selena said, "That dancing fool was into herself, if you ask me. Thought she was all that. Right, bitch?"

Madison said, "Right, bitch. A day drinker, if you ask me. And prob a ho." Selena nodded in approval.

Parrot-beak said, "I know, right?" I'd heard Parrot-beak in the restroom line earlier, agreeing with some other girl, who said the bluff dancer was majorly awesome.

A low buzz vibrated through my mind, like there were bees in my head. I expected somebody to tap me on the shoulder and say, "Hey Star, wasn't that your mom? What in the world was she doing, dancing all by herself up there? By the way, was she really naked?"

I'd only been at this school for a while, this time. I was here for a while in third grade too, and also for a while in the first grade. I'd never even been here for a whole school year at once. But that was no guarantee that nobody would know the bluff dancer was naked and that she was my mother.

I thought about asking to go to the school nurse. I'd say I was sick and that they'd better call Bonnie Sue to come get me. I'd heard they only sent you home if you had a fever, though. But then I'd also heard that if you sucked on a penny, you'd show a fever on the thermometer, whether you had one or not. I wish I knew if it was true.

Ree always said to stay away from authorities because they were nothing but trouble. Authorities had caused trouble for us before, that was for sure. And Ree's warning would include going to the school nurse, since Ree's warning included going to school at all, in the first place. I was in a complicated situation.

Thank god the horror show school day ended before I could make up my mind about the nurse. It was Friday, so maybe everybody would forget about Ree by Monday. Ree might come and take me away by then, anyway.

I wished Ree could just move in too, at my dad and Bonnie Sue's house. But that was a babyish wish. Only somebody like Brynn would think that might really happen. Ree could live near us though, if she wanted to. Then I wouldn't have to start all over somewhere new again. But Ree didn't like cities, or even towns. Not for long, anyway.

The bell rang for us car riders to leave. When I got outside, I spotted Bonnie Sue's red Kia Rio in the line with all the other waiting cars but Bonnie Sue wasn't in it. She was under the cottonwood trees, where she liked to hang out with some other mothers while they waited. I caught her eye and waved. I stayed by the car, hoping she'd come right away, before any bluff dancer chisme got to her.

She rushed right over, smiling with her big Chiclet teeth and I felt sorry for her. Ree was back, so she'd come and get me soon and then Bonnie Sue would be supersonic sad. It gave me that slinky feeling in my stomach again. More trouble. And guess who'd be right in the middle of that trouble, too? That's right. Me, Star Garza.

Ree said Bonnie Sue was domestic livestock, too stupid to even know she was trapped in a pen. That's what Ree said about everybody who had a normal life, though.

Bonnie Sue was super nice to me. She'd even quit her job at Hobby Lobby so she could "take care of you-know-whosie." That's what she kept telling people. I sort of liked being the you-know-whosie. But it was also sort of embarrassing that Bonnie Sue had the idea that I was some big whoop type girl who she should make such a big deal over, when I was really just the regular model, if even that.

"How was your day, sugar britches?" Bonnie Sue said, when we were in the car and on our way home to her and my dad's house. She was from Kentucky, where they said things like sugar britches and didn't mean anything pervy by it.

"Okay, I guess." When your mother and stepmom didn't get along, you learned to keep your pie hole shut. Pie hole was another Kentucky saying that's not meant in a dirty way.

At home, I started on my homework at the kitchen table, while Bonnie Sue fixed my snack: a glass of milk and some of the licorice-flavored biscochitos that we'd made the night before.

Bonnie Sue said biscochitos were the state cookie of New Mexico. I liked chocolate chip cookies with pecans better. Peanut butter cookies came in second. I'd say biscochitos were tied for third place though, with oatmeal raisin cookies. Now she said, "I got a cute idea, when you're finished there."

"What? What is it?" Bonnie Sue had a lot of ideas and some of them were pretty cool.

"Oh, all right. I reckon I can go ahead and show you now," she said, leaving the room. She came back with some fabric, blue with tiny pink octopi all over it. She held it up, along with a sewing pattern. "Let's make you a cute little octopus skirt for church. We can do your hair up like an octopus, too. See, we'll put a ponytail on top of your head, then do it into eight braids from there, hanging down in all different directions. I saw it in a magazine at the hairdresser's.

"Wait 'til Big Mom-Mom sees this!" She clapped her hands together, excited, then covered her mouth. We had to be quiet because my dad was sleeping. He worked the graveyard shift at the mozzarella plant.

Big Mom-Mom was my grandmother, my dad's mother. Big Mom-Mom's backyard backed up to Bonnie Sue and my dad's backyard, so it was like one giant, double backyard. Or one big domestic livestock pen, as Ree put it.

Big Mom-Mom used to be like best friends with Ree, though I was too young to remember it. Me, Ree and my dad had lived with Big Mom-Mom. But now Big Mom-Mom was best friends with Bonnie Sue. They'd walk right into each other's houses; they didn't even knock.

They were as close as Selena and Madison at school. It would be so funny if Bonnie Sue and Big Mom-Mom started calling each other "bitch" all the time. But they only said things like "goldarnit" and "blooming."

Bonnie Sue held up a pair of dangly octopus earrings, with itty-bitty blue gems for eyes. I squealed, then remembered my dad was sleeping and covered my mouth, to show that I recognized my mistake.

Bonnie Sue and Big Mom-Mom had taken me to get my ears pierced at Claire's Boutique at the mall for my eleventh birthday back in February, after I begged and begged. They bought me trainer bras on the same trip but I was so scared and excited about getting my ears pierced that I barely even noticed the bras at the time. Earrings were just about my favorite thing in the whole world.

Bonnie Sue was still standing there, holding up the stuff for the octopus project, like she hadn't understood my happy squeal. So I said, "Cool!" which seemed to make her very happy.

#

When Bonnie Sue and my dad had to come get me this last time, the trouble had really started a few weeks before that, on New Year's Eve. Me and Ree had been staying with Ree's boyfriend Hal in his mobile home in Hobbs, and he wanted to throw a New Year's Eve party, or a "shin-dig," as he called it. I pictured people digging up dirt and standing in it up to their shins but it didn't make any sense.

Ree was in a great mood the day of the party. She played music on her phone, switching back and forth between rock and country, and that chanting and drumming stuff she liked. She stuck the phone inside a plastic cup, placed on its side on the kitchen counter, so the sound carried. Me and Ree danced around the mobile home all day, cleaning house and fixing the party food, like normal people. We made slow cooker cocktail weenies and miniature sandwiches and stuff.

Ree only ate plain food, herself. Like, she might have a piece of baked chicken but not fried chicken or a chicken sandwich with the white bread, cheese and mayonnaise. Or she'd eat a baked potato with salt but no French fries or potato chips, and like that.

So, we also had to fix a raw fruit, vegetable and nut tray for Ree, though she said everybody else could have some of it, too. Ree said anything too far off from its natural state made her sick to her stomach because she was used to her time free, when she'd live off the land.

Hal brought in a stack of boxes of canned beer, practically piled to the top of his head. He said, "Ah, there it is. I wondered if you fixed your natural food plate yet."

Ree turned the music up instead of answering him because he'd start off with a regular comment like that, and then he'd make fun of you. That was one thing about Hal. He liked to call people out when nobody asked his opinion.

He said, "You're still living off the land, I see. Oh, wait. I didn't know my name was "The Land.""

Ree ignored him again. After a while, he gave up on razzing her and took the beers out of the cases, cramming as many as he could into the fridge. After he finished, Ree took them all back out again. We needed the space to keep the party food cold.

Hal griped and flapped around the living room about that. But then he finally went out again, to buy some ice for keeping the beer cold. Ree and I pulled a face at each other, about how annoying and dumb he was. It was me and her against hamster head Hal.

A bunch of people came to the party, almost all grown-ups. But one lady brought her kids. She brought a girl who was a year older than me and a boy who was a year younger than me. So I fit right in the middle. I was jazzed to have other kids around and took them straight to my bedroom. I snatched the Jenga and mancala games off the coffee table on the way. The three of us played games and snuck beer and cigarettes. As Bonnie Sue would have said, it was a hoot and they were toots.

After a while, the grown-ups pushed the furniture against the living room walls and started dancing. The two kids were named Alejandra and Alejandro, but they went by

"Ah-ha" and "Uh-oh." We had a blast, going out into the hallway to spy on the grown-ups, then going back to my room to make fun of them.

An old man with a long gray beard danced like he was playing hopscotch. He kept his arms straight down at his sides. Then a big lady and her super skinny partner started dancing nasty. She had her whole leg up, wrapped around his waist, even though she had a dress on. You could see her lime-green unders.

The big lady said, "I'm going back, baby. I'm going back," like she was some big deal on *Dancing with the Stars* or something. She did a one-legged backbend type move and fell to the floor, a hard thump that shook the whole trailer. But the funniest part was the surprised look on her face and the weird sound she made, like "Onk!"

I ran back to the bedroom with Ah-ha and Uh-oh and we fell all over each other, laughing our heads off. Ah-ha said, "Ooh, look at me, baby. Look at me. Onk, baby. Onk!" She flopped back onto my bed and waggled her leg in the air.

As the night went on, the grown-ups got drunker and louder and then this one man threw up all over the stove. It was thin, clear vomit with lumps in it, all under the stove burners and everything. I only peeked for a second, then ran back to my bedroom to report on it, before any grown-ups got the idea to try to make me clean it up.

At midnight, somebody went outside and fired a gun up in the air. Me, Ah-ha and Uh-oh hunched down in my bedroom closet together. When we finally got brave enough to sneak out into the hallway again, some blonde lady with a laugh like a machine gun was sitting on Hal's lap.

Ree came into my bedroom doorway and motioned to me. She said, "It's time to go." It made me supersonic mad. I'd finally just found friends, who I was hoping would be my new *best* friends. I'd also finally got my bedroom fixed up just right. That took weeks of keeping an eye out for things I could use. I had striped beach towels as curtains, seashells on top of the dresser and a life preserver hanging on the wall. I was pretty proud of my cool beach bedroom. Whenever you went in there, you'd leave boring Hobbs far behind.

But Ree made me shoo Ah-ha and Uh-oh out of the bedroom and then I had to bundle up my clothes and stuff and hand them out to Ree, through the bedroom window. She grabbed them from the outside and put them in our ugly old van.

We couldn't sneak off anyway because somebody was parked behind our van in the driveway. We had to wait until they left. I called Ah-ha and Uh-oh back into my room but the mood was gone. It was after two in the morning before Ree and I could sneak away.

Ree didn't turn the headlights on until we were a couple of blocks away from Hal's. I said, "But why do we have to go?" Maybe it was because the party got so crazy. But the party was just about over now.

Ree said, "Because I come from the Irish Travelers, and travelling is what we do."

"Well, Big Mom-Mom said she didn't think you really did come from the Irish Travelers. Besides, you said you grew up by yourself, in the Blue Ridge Mountains of West Virginia."

Ree said, "Big Mom-Mom is domestic livestock. She's Big Moo-Moo."

"I saw a lady sit on Hal's lap but he didn't want her there. He tried to push her off." He didn't try to push her off but I didn't care. I just wanted to go back there. Ree sighed, like

I was the one who was ruining her life when it was the other way around.

She said, "Listen kid, when a man starts acting the way he has lately, it's gone wooden. It's over."

"Wooden" was Ree's word for things being stiff and still, like how wood is a dead tree or something like that. Whenever Ree started talking about things going wooden, it meant we'd be moving on.

"But you said your parents dragged you all over the place when they were on the run from the law, and you hated it. Well, I hate it, too. What about me?" Ree had lots of different stories about how she'd been raised.

She laughed, but not in a happy way. She said, "Yeah, what about you. Anyway, we're in the waning moon, the time for endings. It's time. Now quit arguing with me or I'll smack you. I don't know what's got into you lately. You're probably going to start your period soon, Hailey Hormones."

I climbed behind the seats, where Ree couldn't reach me while she was driving. I was still mad and felt like getting on her nerves. I said, "What happens if we leave when there's a full moon, then? Do we turn into pumpkins?"

"Quit it. You know the moon phases are just another way of telling time. There's a time for everything and right now, it is time to go."

"Why can't you just find ways to make things less wooden at Hal's, instead of us having to leave?"

"Hush up. Fix me a smoke."

I dug around in Ree's pouch for her smoking stuff, packed some tobacco into the pipe and handed it to her. I still felt like bothering her. I said, "Smoking isn't natural. Why don't you just eat the tobacco? That would be more natural." Ree deserved to have to eat the tobacco.

"You sound just like Halibut. Want me to take you back there and leave you there? Because I will. I'll turn around right now and give you to Halitosis."

I didn't say anything else because knowing Ree, she might really do it. I lay down on the carpeted floor of the van, behind the two rows of seats. I faced the back doors, keeping my crying to myself.

#

I wanted to sleep in the van, at least, but nope, Ree just had to make us sleep in the cave. She went on and on, like it was the greatest thing in the world to sleep in a cold, dark hole in the world. The coffee can candles didn't keep us as warm as they did in the van, since the cave was bigger than the van and open to the outdoors, too. And here in the cave, with nobody else around, anything or anybody could just come in and get us. Mountain lions or outlaws could walk right in, while we were sleeping.

But Ree didn't care. Every evening, she'd park somewhere off the main road and we'd have to carry our sleeping bags to the cave. We'd carry them back to the van again early the next morning. You weren't allowed in there without permission but Ree said nobody owned the wilderness. They just thought they did.

It was warmer in the cave than it was outside at least, but you still had to stuff yourself way down into your sleeping bag and stay there all night, aside from if you had to get up and go do your business outside. And there were more hours of darkness than you'd want to sleep through too, so it got supersonic boring.

Ree shined the flashlight around the cave, laying on her back in her sleeping bag. She said, "Just think, thousands and thousands of years ago, people slept right here, just like we are now. You can bet they did. They knew it was a great sleeping spot, the same as we do. Isn't that fascinating?"

She held the flashlight still when it lit on a clump of small bats. They look like creepy science fiction mice. I slept with my head all the way inside the sleeping bag every night, in case a bat might un-hibernate and land on me. "Bats carry rabies," I said.

"We'll see about that. You're doing a paper on bats tomorrow. Find out what kind of bats these are and their habits. Two pages, minimum."

I had to watch what I said around Ree. She was liable to give me an assignment on whatever I brought up, especially if I was getting on her nerves.

She said, "Also, you could work on your personality. You used to be so sweet. Nobody likes a negative Nancy, you know."

Coyotes started yipping. It was like the beginning of a horror movie, like we were getting signs that doom was on the way, with the creepy bats and the coyotes yipping at the moon. I scrunched down into my sleeping bag until it covered my whole head.

Ree shined the flashlight on me. "Hey, you. Come out of there. That's just a bunch of men howling at the moon. It must be closing time at the bar." She laughed, then sat up and started doing her yipping call back. The coyotes answered. She did it again, *Ruh-ray-ooo, yip, yip.*

"Stop it! They'll come in here."

"So what? Let 'em. Don't be a chicken Chelsea. *Yip, yip, ruh-ray-ooo.* "

The coyotes returned her call again. It reminded me of when I played kickball with some kids at a park at one of the places we stayed, and Ree had called me home with her coyote yip.

The kids started laughing and copying Ree's call, "Yip, yip, ruh-ray-ooo, Star Garza shits coy-dog poo!" Then it turned into them saying I ate coy-dog poo, too. Then, I actually was coy-dog poo.

After that, they called me "Coy-dog Garza." The only good thing about moving around all the time was that you got to leave the bad things behind, too.

#

After days and days of Ree making me sleep in the cave and study in the van during the day, I couldn't stand anymore of it. I said, "This is the most wooden place in the world. Nowhere else on earth could ever be as wooden as this."

Ree didn't like that. She thought living like a wild thing was heaven on earth. She looked up from her book, *The Philosophy of Andy Warhol*. When there was no TV, Ree and I read just about anything we could find. We'd load up on books from thrift shops, a whole big boxful at a time. She said, "Oh yeah? How would you like some excitement like a butt whipping with a wooden switch? Or maybe you'd rather have the excitement of being dropped off at the wooden CYFD office? You'd appreciate me then."

"Why can't you just be normal?" There. I said it.

Ree started yelling that I wasn't her daughter and that she didn't even know me anymore. I stopped speaking to her after that, since I wasn't supposed to talk to strangers.

By lunch time, Ree was going crazy at the silent treatment I gave her. She stopped threatening and started begging. She tossed *Andy Warhol* aside and said, "All right, all right. We'll go to town then, grumpy Gretchen. Will that make you happy?"

I looked up from Ree's phone and the notebook I was writing in. Ree was making me write a booklet about the area. I'd just finished ringtails and was about to start on cave pearls. Sometimes, like now, I'd be able to look stuff up on Ree's phone, even out in the middle of nowhere. Other times, I couldn't. I didn't bring it up to Ree because then she might make me write a paper about that, too.

"Yes," I answered. Going to town *would* make me happy. I didn't know if Ree meant we were going to live in town for a while or just go there for a couple of hours, though. I didn't ask because saying the wrong thing could make her get stubborn again. I hoped she'd find a man in town. Ree was proud of never paying any rent, so when there was no man to pay our way, we'd have to stay somewhere free, even if we had money. Ree called it our time free, like it was something good.

Ree's mood got better. She took her phone back and played some music on it, then poured us each a cup of her kitchen wine, which she made from fruit juice and bread. She said, "Go on and put some snow in these drinks while I get our stuff together." I scooped snow into our cups. The wine was sour, like nasty cold medicine, but I drank it anyway because I knew I'd feel more calm and happy with a little buzz on.

We stopped at a gas station. After filling up the tank, we went to the ladies' room to take better sponge baths than we could in the van. Ree poured herself another drink first, and brought it along. She never let me have more than one.

After washing her hair in the sink, she crouched under the hand dryer on the wall to dry it. Her hair got a lot of notice. It was coppery orange-colored and long enough that the ends of it touched the floor when she bent over.

We stocked up on supplies at the grocery store, then washed our clothes at a laundromat. Ree kept looking up from *Andy Warhol* to say, "What a treat," like sitting in a hard chair at the laundromat was living high. On time free, we usually let our dirty clothes soak in a bucket of soapy water and rinsed them in a bucket of plain water. Then we'd wring them out and hang them up to dry. Since it was winter, we could only wash a few things at a time. That's all we had room to hang around the inside of the van during the day, when we were in there with the coffee can candles, with Ree reading and me studying.

After our clothes were clean and folded, we drove to some big metal building. The sign called it a pool hall, though it had more than just pool tables. It also had a dance floor and a bar, and best of all, a restaurant. I said, "After we eat, can we go find a mall?"

"You don't need to go to a mall."

That made me mad all over again. I said, "Everything's always for you," because it was. The barmaid came by and I ordered the country fried steak with mashed potatoes and a chocolate shake. I didn't even care that Ree was staring me down for not asking her permission first. I was surprised that she didn't say anything, though. She just let me get it.

Ree ordered the fish, broiled dry, with a plain baked potato, a salad with no dressing or cheese and water with a lemon wedge. The barmaid rolled her eyes.

"She's jealous of me," Ree said, like the lady wasn't standing right there.

Ree always thought other women were jealous of her, especially if they weren't built as good as she was. But really, it was weird to be all picky about every little thing when you ate at a restaurant, like you were too special to eat what everybody else ate. I said, "How about Walmart then, at least?"

"No. We just went shopping. We don't have the money or room for a bunch of junk we don't need."

"I just feel like going somewhere that's for kids, too. How about a movie? Or maybe a skating rink or something?"

"No. And stop always asking for more, more, more. Just quit, goddammit."

She was getting super mad so I stopped. I watched a family at another table, a real family with a mom and a dad, and a brother and sister. They were talking and laughing together, like a TV family. I bet those kids would get to go to the mall after they ate. They probably got to go everywhere.

I cheered up when the food came. The crispy chicken fried steak was amazing. So were the garlicky mashed potatoes and the shake with whipped cream and a cherry on top. I never tasted anything so great in my whole life. But after I ate, I got terrible tummy cramps and had to rush to the bathroom.

When I came back, Ree looked happy. She said, "There now, you see? All that garbage food made you sick. That's what you get. Next thing you knew, you'd be all fattened up for slaughter, like the rest of the domestic livestock."

I narrowed my eyes at her.

She said, "If this smart-ass attitude is any hint of what you're going to be like as a teenager…Well, I just don't know."

Ree paid the check, so I thought we were leaving. But, nope. After that, she went to the jukebox, picked out some songs, and started her slow man-call sway on the dance floor. The place was about half full but it was still light outside and nobody else was dancing.

She spun around, her long fiery hair catching male interest in the darkened room. She did that thing where she slowly touched herself with her arms crossed, ankles, knees, and on to her hips and shoulders. Then she'd toss her hair. At least in here, she kept her clothes on.

I was disappointed. I didn't want to just sit here all night, even though it was better than being stuck in the van or the cave. But if Ree found a decent man, that would be a ton better than just one little stop at the movies or the mall. I got the keys out of Ree's pouch and went to the van for my drawing stuff and the book I was reading, *Charlotte's Web.*

When I came back in, a man was dancing with Ree, or dancing next to her, at least. Then another man got up there, too. "Dancing in the Dark" ended and a song I didn't know came on.

The barmaid brought me an icy mug of root beer. She said, "Oh, there you are. Hard to see back here in this corner booth. Here, I brung you a sodie. I got a little girl about your age. Her name's Amber." The barmaid looked at Ree on the dance floor, with three men dancing around her now, and shook her head.

One of the men kind of shoved one of the other men. Ree just kept dancing because it's normal for the male of the species to fight for breeding rights. Anybody who's spent much time free could tell you that. I wished the barmaid would stop shaking her head and go away. How would she like it if I shook my head about her mother, right in front of her.

I thought of connected words like *bar, barmaid, barrette, em-bar-rassed, bare-assed.* I picked up Ree's phone and looked up "bar," but it had too many definitions to make sense as a word root. When I looked up again, the nosy barmaid was gone.

I searched for stuff on Ree's phone that I wished I could have. If Ree found a man, maybe I could get some of it, or even all of it. You never knew. I wanted a bedroom with a daybed that made the room seem like its own little living room. It would be covered with a bedspread that had red hearts on it. Then I saw a picture of a bedroom that had a miniature refrigerator, like in a motel room. That would be supersonic cool, like having my own apartment. I forgot to breathe for a second, thinking that might be possible. I also wanted a phone of my own, a bike and a necklace made special with my initials. I wanted swimming pool, some perfume and a cat. Those were the main things.

I was there a long time. I drew a bedroom-apartment, with a cat laying on the heart-covered daybed covers. I read a few more chapters of *Charlotte's Web*.

Ree sat at a table with some people. Then she danced with one guy, then another guy. Finally, she was having a drink at a different table, just her and one man now. Maybe I'd get to live in a real home again right away, and then I could find a best friend. Sleepy now, I lay down in the booth, thinking about what color cat to get. I planned to name it after a fancy, faraway place like Morocco or Paducah.

I woke to super bright lights. Everybody was gone, except the barmaid, who was mopping the floor. She jumped a little when I sat up. "Oh! I didn't see you," she said. "Where's your mother?" At the same time, I said, "Where's my mother?"

I said, "Jinx!"

The barmaid didn't laugh, though. She just leaned on her mop and shook her head. I pictured her shaking her head so much that it finally rolled off her neck and plopped into the bucket of mop water. Her hair looked like a mop, too.

I ran out the door but the parking lot was mostly empty. Our van was gone.

Back inside, Ree's pouch was gone, too. So was her phone. I said, "I'll just wait here."

"Well, you cain't, honey. I'm about to close up for the night. I cain't leave you in here by yourself."

"I'll wait outside, then." I tried to get out the door again but the barmaid blocked it.

"Oh no, you don't. I cain't leave you outside by yourself at 2:30 in the morning. You're just a little kid."

A chill crawled up my back, like a cold, creepy-crawly thing from the cave. Ree had ditched me again.

I didn't appreciate her enough and now she was gone. I wished more than anything for another chance. I wouldn't complain or always ask for more.

The barmaid said, "Who should I call to come and get you?"

I said, "Nobody can come and get me." Telling her anything would be about the same as snitching to the authorities because it could be used against Ree. I said, "My mother just forgets about the time, sometimes. She's like a big kid, ha ha."

The barmaid didn't laugh or even smile. She was a sour Sarah who needed to work on her personality. She rinsed the mop in her big bucket, then lit a cigarette. I felt my heart flip over in my chest.

She took a long drag, then said, "Alrighty, then. You can come on home with me. But if we don't find your mother by the time my shift starts tomorrow evening, then we're gonna have to do something different. I could get in a ton of trouble for this, as it is."

She put on her coat and said, "Wait here while I warm up the car. And remember, I'm doing you a big favor, kiddo. Try to run off again and I'll call the cops on you and your mother both. Got it?"

"Yes, ma'am," I said, being extra polite.

After the car was warmed up, the barmaid came back to get me. On our way out, she taped a note outside the pool hall door. She said it was a note with her phone number and address on it, for my mother. I was glad she'd heated up her car because I'd left my hat and gloves in the van. She said to call her Charla.

Her house was only a few blocks away. It looked like a square face, with two window eyes and a door nose. The doorstep was the face house's mouth. After we got inside, Charla said her daughter and the babysitter were asleep. She made up a bed for me on the sofa.

She said, "Alrighty now hon, what's your mother's name? We better call the hospital and the jail--- I mean, I'm sure your mother just forgot about the time but we ought to check anyway. Just to put our minds at rest."

"I don't know my mother's name. I just call her Mother." I really didn't know Ree's phone number. Ree wouldn't want me to give it out anyway.

Charla asked again, louder, like she was mad. I tried not to cry.

She said, "Christ on a cracker," and lit another cigarette. I stayed quiet and still, like an invisible girl who wouldn't be any trouble at all to have around. I worried that she'd changed her mind and call the cops.

She said, "Alrighty, then. I'll be in that bedroom right there if you need anything. Nighty-night, kiddo." She went in the bedroom and shut the door.

When I woke up, the sun streamed in through the window. I wondered if Ree had called Charla. Charla could have slept through the call. A girl was at the kitchen table, eating cereal. She said, "My name's Amber. I'm nine. Do your parents know you're here?"

The kid was nosy, like her mother. I said, "I'm Star. My mother will be here soon."

"How old are you?"

I said, "Twelve." I was almost eleven.

Amber helped me get breakfast. They had a whole pantry shelf full of cereal to pick from: Cocoa Krispies, Apple Jacks, Golden Grahams. I felt nearly as thrilled as when I'd snuck cigarettes with Ah-ha and Uh-oh on New Year's Eve. Ree didn't allow sugary breakfast cereal. I picked the Froot Loops, because of their beautiful Hawaiian colors.

After breakfast, we played Barbies and watched cartoons. Amber seemed babyish for her age but Ree said domestic livestock kids were dumber than kids who'd spent much time free. They needed babysitters because they were weak and stupid. It was true but Amber was okay anyway.

Charla and the babysitter came out of the bedrooms at about the same time. Amber's babysitter was grandma aged, which seemed weird. I thought babysitters were supposed to be teenagers. Charla told Amber and me to take turns taking our baths. She said I'd have to put on my same clothes again and to use my finger for a toothbrush.

After that, Amber and I played with Play-Doh. I made a cat and then a hard-boiled egg that was white on the outside and yellow on the inside. Amber made a horse or a dog. Then we played a card game called War. It was fun to hang out in a house. I'd forget about Ree for a while, then I'd remember again and my stomach would drop. I was in the middle of trouble again.

Later, we had hot dogs with mustard and ketchup and they were wonderful. But then the too-old babysitter came over again and I had to go back to the pool hall with Charla. I didn't want to go.

Charla's note was still taped to the outside of the pool hall door. She pulled it off and stuck it in her pocket. When we got inside, she said, "Alrighty, this is it. You got to give me somebody to call right now or I'm gonna have to call the cops. Sorry, kid."

I told her my dad was Frank Garza in Roswell, and that my stepmom's name was Bonnie Sue. Charla gave me a long look, because I'd lied. And now Ree would be mad at me too, because I'd stopped lying.

#

An hour and a half later, Bonnie Sue and my dad pulled up in my dad's truck. Bonnie Sue kept hugging me and asking me questions, like I was practically a victim of kidnapping or something. It was like she wanted to make Ree's mistake out to be the crime of the century, in front of everybody. It made me feel even worse.

Bonnie Sue and my dad had rushed over here as soon as Charla called. Bonnie Sue even stopped in the middle of frying a chicken. We ate there at the pool hall, before heading to Roswell. My last meal here was only yesterday but it seemed like a lot longer than that. I got the chicken fried steak with mashed potatoes and a chocolate shake again because it might be a long time before I got that chance again. It didn't make me sick this time.

After I was in bed, back in my old room at Bonnie Sue and my dad's house, I heard them arguing in their bedroom. Bonnie Sue was arguing, anyway. My dad didn't really argue. He mostly just seemed like he was about to fall asleep.

Bonnie Sue said, "Frank. We've got to do something. That lunatic drifter trash cannot be trusted with this precious child again. It just ain't right."

My dad talked slow, with his Mexican accent. "When we're needed, we go. See?" I had never seen my dad even get mad, so I don't know why Ree called him Frankenstein.

"Frank." Bonnie Sue's voice got quieter but higher-pitched, like she was crying but trying not to wake me up.

After a while, my dad's voice again, "Eet looks brighter mañana. Jest go to sleep, mama."

Later still, he turned the TV on low in the living room. I heard him open the fridge, then crack open a can of beer. He was used to staying up all night because of his work hours. I almost got up too, since I couldn't sleep anyway. But it seemed like it wouldn't be allowed here, for me to be up so late. I'd already caused enough trouble for one day.

I thought about my bedroom here, what I might be able to do with it, even though I didn't think I'd be here for very long at all. I might not even be here for more than just tonight. But if it was longer than that for some reason, maybe Bonnie Sue would help me fix it up, just for something fun to do. It was pink and frilly and there was a dollhouse in the corner. It was a little kid's room.

#

Bonnie Sue called Hobby Lobby and quit her job the next morning. She was on the phone with her boss when Big Mom-Mom came through the back door. Bonnie Sue quit her job because I was there, before I got a chance to tell her she shouldn't, since I probably wouldn't even be here for long.

Big Mom-Mom gave me a giant hug, then picked me up and twirled me around. She said, "My goodness. I missed you so much! We all did. We were so, so worried about you." I felt bad about that but I didn't know what to say. I hadn't talked to any of them since the last time I was here, two years ago. Ree didn't allow it. She said they'd only try to pump me for information to use against her.

I guess Big Mom-Mom wasn't too mad at me though, because after she set me back down, she pinched my cheeks. She said, "And just look at you! You're practically all grown up! And what a pretty young lady you are." Then she went into the kitchen and poured herself a cup of coffee. She poured Bonnie Sue a cup, too. She said, "And how about some café con leche with a little cinnamon, for this grown-up girl here?"

I said. "Okay. Thanks." I hadn't liked café con leche that much the last time I was here, but I liked being offered a special drink that was just for me.

Bonnie Sue, off the phone now, said to me, "Now, I was thinking about calling my friend from the Hobby Lobby, Miss Annette. Her daughter Brynn is in the same grade as you. I thought we could ask Brynn to help you out with going back to school here. Let's invite them over for pizza tonight. Okay?"

I definitely wanted some pizza and I loved to hang out with other kids. School though, that was way too many kids at once. School was too much. I said, "Can't I keep homeschooling here with you? I mean, if, for some reason, Ree doesn't come back right away?" That was also a hint to Bonnie Sue not to expect me to be here for long. Her, my dad and Big Mom-Mom were all super nice but they weren't who I belong to.

Bonnie Sue seemed to think the idea of homeschooling me was hilarious. She said, "Honey, I wouldn't have the first idea how to do that. You're way too smart for me already!" Big Mom-Mom laughed, too. If Ree didn't show up soon, I'd be sunk.

Miss Annette and Brynn came over that night. Brynn was nice but she seemed even more babyish than that Amber girl, and Amber was only nine. Brynn's hair was in baby pigtails up high up on her head and she brought coloring books and crayons with her, in a pink plastic little kid's backpack. She sat there at the table, coloring like a kindergartener. And she had on light green pants and a matching top, with little bunnies all over them, a total baby outfit.

#

When Bonnie Sue drove Brynn and me to school a couple of days later, I felt like crying, even before we pulled up in front of the building. *Where was Ree? What if she was dead?*

I didn't remember the school being so big, from the last time I was here, two years ago. I was glad Brynn was with me, at least. Bonnie Sue had called the principal ahead of time and he said they had room for me in Brynn's class, with Mr. Villalobos.

Bonnie Sue said, "Don't you worry, honey pie. You just stick with Brynn today. She'll show you around. Won't you, sweetie?"

"Yes, ma'am," Brynn said.

Bonnie Sue said, to me, "See? Easy as pie. And then you and me will start on that bedroom, as soon as I pick you up this afternoon."

Brynn would ride the bus home this afternoon, like she usually did. She only rode with us this morning because Bonnie Sue asked her to, for my first day.

Throughout the day I'd think, okay, only six more hours until I could get out of here and start re-doing my bedroom. Then five hours, then three. Bonnie Sue packed Brynn and me identical lunches. She put Hostess cherry pies and surprise cherry lip balms in our lunch bags.

Brynn said, "Goody gumdrops! Miss Bonnie Sue is so nice. And see, you made it halfway through the day already. You're doing great." Brynn was pretty nice, herself.

#

"Can you call Charla again?" I said to Bonnie Sue, as we sat down to a Mexican dinner.

"That's Miss Charla to you, Miss. And I don't believe we should keep bothering her."

"But maybe she saw Ree. Maybe she saw her and forgot to tell us."

"No, punkin' pie, I don't think that's very likely at all. Like I told you, I talk to Miss Charla every couple of weeks. She said she'll be sure to call if she sees or hears anything. And I know that she will." I wondered if Charla and Bonnie Sue trash talked Ree together. I bet they did.

"But can you just call her one more time, then that'll be it for a while? Please?" We were all at Big Mom-Mom's house for dinner. Big Mom-Mom made a sad face.

Bonnie Sue said, "Oh, all right. One more time. But that's it." She called but Charla didn't answer her phone.

Bonnie Sue left a message. Then she said, "Miss Charla is probably at work. I'm sure your biological mother is fine."

"Thanks," I said. I meant for calling Charla, not for calling Ree my biological mother or saying she was fine, when we didn't know that at all.

My dad kept eating his enchiladas.

"Ain't that right, Frank?" Bonnie Sue said.

"Eet's great. Love thees Christmas chile!"

Bonnie Sue said, a little loud, "I'm not talking about enchiladas with red and green chile sauce, Frank. I'm talking about your daughter trying to get reassurance that her---biological mother is ali—okay."

"Eet's okay. Don' worry."

Bonnie Sue caught Big Mom-Mom's gaze and rolled her eyes.

Big Mom-Mom looked down at her plate, like she wasn't even getting into this one.

Bonnie Sue said to me, "Your job, Miss Star, is to worry about your life as an eleven-year-old, and let the grown-ups worry about grown-up stuff like that. Okay?"

"Okay," I said, though it didn't even make any sense. Who wouldn't worry, when their mother was missing?

Bonnie Sue said, "Remember, if Ree comes back but you'd rather stay here, that's fine too, sugar. In fact, your daddy and I think that would be for the best. Ain't that right, Frank?"

My dad said, "Si."

"Why do you talk like that?" I said. I wasn't trying to be rude, I just wondered. Big Mom-Mom was white and she didn't say "ees" and "eet's." She said "is" and "it's." Well, maybe I was trying to be rude, a little. It was like Bonnie Sue getting mad at him was contagious and now I was mad at him, too. His calmness could get on your nerves. It was like I was Bonnie Sue's kid and he was just some guy, anyway.

He looked up, like he was surprised, then wiped his mustache off with his napkin. He said, "Okay."

That didn't answer my question at all, so Bonnie Sue started laughing and then I joined in. Even Big Mom-Mom laughed. She said, "When he was a little boy, you could set him on the sofa and if you came back three days later, he'd still be right there where you left him."

My dad said, "My ladies have all thee personality. None left for poor Frank Garza."

Big Mom-Mom said to me, "About the speech differences, dear, your daddy's father and stepfather were both Mexican. Your daddy talks like them, only with a whole lot more English. We lived in Mexico for years. You didn't know that?"

I didn't remember if I ever knew that or not. I only even remembered I was part Mexican myself when a real Mexican would talk to me in Spanish, like they thought I'd know the language.

#

My month of having to wear the starter earrings was up and now I could wear different ones every day of the week, if I felt like it. I already had ten pairs, on the heart-shaped earring tree Bonnie Sue gave me for Valentine's Day, which is two days after my birthday. I picked the little yellow star earrings and then looked at myself in them, in my wall mirror. Today the red paint me and Bonnie Sue put on my old dresser should be dry. I twirled around in my bedroom.

I felt like a princess here, on some days. Other days, it was too much and made me cranky. Ree's attention wasn't on me all the time like Bonnie Sue's was, even when Ree and I had been stuck together in the van all day.

Bonnie Sue popped her head into my room, like she did at least every thirty minutes. She said, "Miss Annette just called. Brynn is coming over after a while. She'll be spending the night. Her mama's got a big date with her new man."

Brynn could never stay home alone, not even during the daytime. And she didn't even know that the grown-ups sent her over here so they could fuck. I had to explain it to her. And even then, she didn't believe me. At least I made her stop wearing her hair in those baby pigtails. I was trying to make her get her ears pierced too but she was too much of a scaredy-cat. I'd rather hang out with Selena but she was always with Madison, who didn't like me.

Bonnie Sue said Madison was probably just afraid of being left out, and that I should invite both Selena and Madison over for pizza. So I did but they both made excuses and didn't come. I wondered if it was because Bonnie Sue had made me invite Brynn, too. On the other hand, at least Brynn showed up when you invited her over.

Bonnie Sue and Big Mom-Mom were supposed to take me to the fabric store today. Now that Bonnie Sue had taught me to sew bookmarks and hair scrunchies, we were moving on to zippered pouches. After we picked out some fabric remnants, the three of us were supposed to go to lunch at the McDonald's that was shaped like a flying saucer.

In Roswell, there were alien statues and spaceship statues outside businesses and perched on roofs. Stuffed alien toys and t-shirts were for sale everywhere, too. Bonnie Sue had taken me and Brynn to the alien museum twice already, since I'd been back here this time. Bonnie Sue just loved aliens.

I said, "Brynn's coming over? What about the fabric store and McDonald's?"

"Well, that's no problem at all, hon. We'll just bring her along with us."

I loved going places with Big Mom-Mom and Bonnie Sue but one thing I didn't like about being here was that I could never go anywhere by myself. Nowhere at all, except to the big fenced-in pen, Bonnie Sue's and Big Mom-Mom's joined back yards. And even then, I'd have Bonnie Sue looking out at me from one house and Big Mom-Mom looking out at me from the other house.

They said Roswell had gotten really bad with crime, that it wasn't a place for a young girl to go wandering around by herself nowadays. Bonnie Sue and Big Mom-Mom were on the Roswell online group so they knew, they said. Supposedly, Roswell had a higher crime rate than New York City now. They said the whole state was ruined, that drugs had destroyed all the nice towns in New Mexico. I didn't know if it was true or not, though. Ree wasn't afraid to go anywhere. She said if anyone wanted to mess with her, let 'em come on and try it.

I didn't know why Bonnie Sue took away the pocketknife I used to carry in my sock, when she was so worried about my safety. When I asked her, all she'd say was, "That ain't nice."

Now she said, "We've got an hour to spare. Let me show you how to do a zipper." I waited while she set up the sewing machine.

I wondered if there was a word root in there somewhere. "Buttonhole. Butt. Ton. Hole. Butt. On. Hole."

Bonnie Sue stopped what she was doing. She said, "That's no way to talk. Did you learn those words from that Selena girl?"

"No. I mean, no ma'am. Sorry." I didn't realize I was talking out loud. But dang, did Bonnie Sue really think a fifth grader wouldn't know the word butthole? Even Brynn knew that much.

Bonnie Sue looked at me for a long minute and I worried that she had finally noticed I wasn't the big deal she and Big Mom-Mom had thought, after all.

Bonnie Sue got back to showing me how to do a zipper on the sewing machine. Then she said, "Come to think of it, I'll just do the zipper on your skirt myself. You can practice your zippers when we make the pouches. I'm not thinking straight today, sugar plum. Big Mom-Mom saw your biological mother today, ran into her at the gas station. But you don't have to go with her, you know. Your daddy and I really think you ought to stay here with us."

I didn't answer her because I didn't want to hurt her feelings. I slipped off to my bedroom and tried to concentrate on *Are you There God? It's Me, Margaret*, an old book Bonnie Sue or Big Mom-Mom had put on my bookshelf.

The rest of the day was pretty good, picking out pretty fabric remnants, eating at the spaceship McDonald's and hanging out with Brynn. Once in a while, I'd remember that Ree would probably come and get me soon, though. Or that maybe she wouldn't come for me at all. I didn't feel good when I thought of it going either way.

That night, me and Brynn finally got ready to sleep, head to feet on my bed, and I was nodding off. I suddenly felt like someone was staring at me. I opened my eyes, to see an alien face in my window. It was big and pale, with huge black eyes, just like on the alien statues around town. I ran out of my bedroom, screaming for Bonnie Sue.

She rushed out of her room in a thin pink nightie. Her face was covered in night cream, shiny like the alien's. She said, "What is it? What's wrong, honey?"

My dad came out of their bedroom behind her. Brynn came out of my bedroom and stood there too, looking like she was about to cry.

I said, "There was. I saw. I mean, an alien was looking in my window!"

"Mercy! Frank, call the police. I'll call Cheryl." Bonnie Sue hurried to the front door, then the back door, checking that the locks were secured.

She called Big Mom-Mom. "Wake up, Cheryl. Now, don't panic. But grab your gun and check your locks right now, hear? And stay on the phone. There was an alien outside Star's window!"

I huddled with Brynn, too scared to speak anymore.

"I told you, Frank. I told you they was real," Bonnie Sue said, still on the phone with Big Mom-Mom. Bonnie Sue looked almost happy, in a crazed way.

My dad didn't look excited. He looked sleepy, as usual. He said, "I don't think you see an alien. You just eemajeen it."

"Frank!"

"Okay, okay. I check." He started for the front door.

Bonnie Sue said, "Take the gun, Frank!"

"Okay, okay." He went to their bedroom, came out with a handgun and went outside with it.

Bonnie Sue turned off all the inside lights, then followed along with my dad, going from room to room, peeking out through the blinds.

Alien. Alienation. Ailing Nation.

My dad tried to come back in but Bonnie Sue had triple-locked the door. He knocked, then waited on the porch while she flipped on the outdoor light and looked out the peephole.

"I check both houses. Ees no thing," he said, though he was drowned out by all the apologies she kept making, after realizing she'd locked him outside with the alien.

He took Bonnie Sue's phone and said into it, "Eet's okay, Mama. Go back to sleep."

Bonnie Sue glared at him, slitty eyes peering out of her shiny face.

I said, "But I saw…" then stopped. There I was, right at the center of the trouble, like I always was. My dad didn't think it was anything, so maybe it wasn't. Maybe I'd caused all this mess in the middle of the night over nothing.

Bonnie Sue made my dad move my twin mattress into the master bedroom. Me and Brynn were to sleep in their bedroom with them now. After herding us all in there, Bonnie Sue locked the bedroom door, then made my dad push their short, wide dresser in front of it. Then she made him push their tall, narrow dresser in front of the window.

As soon as we were all settled in, Bonnie Sue remembered Big Mom-Mom and made my dad go get her. After that, all five of us slept in the master bedroom. Big Mom-Mom slept on a row of cushions from the sofa.

#

The ladies at church made a big fuss over the octopus skirt that I mostly made by myself, and my octopus hairdo and octopus earrings. Bonnie Sue had tied little pink ribbons at the ends of each of the eight "tentacle" braids that sprouted from the top of my head. I felt sort of stupid but also sort of like I was practically a movie star.

Later, we were finishing up our Sunday pot roast at our house, when Ree's coyote call came through the open window. *Yip, yip, ruh-ray-ooo* she called. *Yip, yip, ruh-ray-ooo.*

"She's back," Big Mom-Mom said, shaking her head and sopping up gravy with a dinner roll, which Bonnie Sue had just corrected me for doing.

"Frank?" Bonnie Sue said, a question that sounded like a warning.

"Por dios," my dad said, nodding like he'd just announced some kind of important and final ruling.

Bonnie Sue tossed her cloth napkin down on the table and got up in a huff, going to answer the door herself.

Ree came in and it was like everybody froze for a minute. It was like that game I played outside in a park with some kids once, where everybody had to freeze in place when the leader said so. Then the leader would try to catch somebody moving, and they'd be out.

My dad would be out because he looked Ree up and down, man-like. It was quick but I saw it. So did Bonnie Sue. Only, instead of telling him he was out of the game, she stepped in between my dad and Ree, blocking his view.

Bonnie Sue said, "Why don't you just leave her here, at least for a while? Listen, she's doing real good in school. She's got a little friend, got her own bedroom. Stability, you know?"

Ree ignored her. She said, "Star, pack up. We leave in five." She looked at the time on her phone.

Under Bonnie Sue's death stare, my dad stood up. He said to Ree, "Let's talk about thees."

Ree said, "Outside then, Frankfurter. By yourself. Star, let's go. Not too much stuff. Two trash bags." She flipped her hair, then went back outside.

My dad stood there with his hands out, like, "Well, what can I do about it?" Then he went outside, after Ree.

Big Mom-Mom said, "Come on, Bonnie Sue. Let's clean up, dear." She started stacking up plates, though we hadn't completely finished eating. Bonnie Sue started gathering dishes from the table, too. She said, in her high pitched but quiet crying voice, "This ain't right. It just ain't right."

I got two trash bags from under the kitchen sink and went to my bedroom to pack, being careful not to look at Bonnie Sue. I felt terrible. Supersonic horrible.

#

Ten minutes after Ree showed up at my dad and Bonnie Sue's house, me and my two trash bags worth of belongings were in the back of the van. Ree drove and some little boy rode shotgun. A man slept beside me on the carpeted van floor, behind the two row of seats. He had long black hair in a braid.

We rode along in silence. I felt like the alien outside my window must have felt, if he was real instead of just in my imagination. I'd been yanked up out of one whole life and plunked down into another life again. Yep, just like a Roswell alien. The bees buzzed like crazy in my head. Like a bee in the bonnet. Word root: Bon. It meant "good," as in bon voyage. *Vagabond, bubonic, bonkers, bonobo, boner.*

After a while, we stopped in a place that had a few small buildings and houses, some of them boarded up. We went into a long, skinny restaurant. A sign on the wall said it used to be a train's dining car. My stomach still felt a little icky but restaurant food was too special to pass up.

After we were seated and had menus, I asked if I could get the chicken fried steak, mashed potatoes and a chocolate shake. I was talking to Ree but the man, whose name was Rex, nodded. Rex and Ree sounded like something you'd name twins. Evil twins. Like *AnoREXia* and *diarRhEEa.*

"She just said 'diarrhea,'" the little boy said, then laughed like somebody was tickling him and wouldn't stop.

"Oh yeah?" Ree said. She reached across the table and started tugging on my octopus braids. As she yanked each braid, she said, "uno puss, dos puss, tres puss," cracking up along with the kid, like calling your daughter puss in front of people was just the funniest thing in the world. Then she went around behind my chair and snapped my bra strap. The little boy laughed some more. Then he came around and snapped my bra strap, too. The man just watched with his big dark eyes, like he was a newly landed alien himself, trying to make sense of this strange new world. I liked him a little better now, for saying I could have the country fried steak when it was an expensive menu item and for not laughing at me, along with Ree and his spoiled brat, who I planned to deal with later.

Ree acted like she was just joking around but she had this thing about my dad and his family. It's like I was a baby bird that fell out of the mama bird's nest and got picked up by others. And now my mama bird was deciding if she'd accept me back or not, after I'd been contaminated. It wasn't fair at all, when Ree was the one who'd pushed me out of her nest in the first place, then flew away. But at least she came back for me. She came back.

It was dark out when we left the restaurant. We stopped for the night soon after that, at an old motel. A super old motel. Each room was a separate little house, shaped like a teepee. Ree and Rex slept in one bed and I had to share the other bed with the little boy. His name was Harley, like the motorcycle. I gave him a hard twisty pinch, for making fun of me earlier.

His face squinched up in pain. Good. That would teach him who he was messing with. After he recovered, he made a mean face back at me. He didn't yell or snitch, though. He wasn't a big baby, at least.

We watched some boring show about Alaska on TV and it was quiet besides that. I'd learned that Rex and Harley were Native, though I didn't know what tribe. The Natives I've known mostly seemed quieter than other people. That was supposed to be a stereotype but they were probably still mad and didn't feel like talking, because of the smallpox thing and how their kids all got shipped off to Indian schools and everything. I wondered if the teepee shaped motel houses or the giant twenty foot tall cartoon Indian chief statue outside the hotel office made Rex mad. If it did, he didn't show it and I didn't ask. Ree still seemed mad at me so I didn't want to call any extra attention to myself.

#

The next day, we had a two hour drive to Albuquerque. There wasn't much to look at on the way. There was just desert on both sides of the road, with clumps of dry grass or a giant rock here and there. I saw a hawk perched on a telephone pole, and a road runner, though. And then there was a pronghorn antelope, wandering around all by itself. I wondered if it was lost. Or maybe it did something to get kicked out of its antelope herd. I'd taken the octopus braids out of my hair before my shower, and tossed the bra and earrings into the bathroom wastebasket, back at the teepee motel room. I tried to de-Bonnie Sue myself so Ree would like me again.

I kept thinking there were big burned patches in the desert up ahead or big holes in the road. But then whenever we'd get closer, the darkened areas lightened up. They were just big shadows from the clouds. Clouds were the only shade around here.

We stopped for a bathroom break. There were a few small boarded up houses around the gas station/convenience store but nothing else as far as I could see. It seemed like there used to be a lot more people in New Mexico than there were now, because there were a lot of abandoned shacks. I had heard that things don't rot in the desert like they do in other places. But it still seemed like there were a weirdly large number of places that people just left.

Why would so many people build houses out in the middle of nowhere, all over New Mexico, then just move away and leave them? I almost asked out loud but then I remembered Ree's love of making me write papers. Sometimes I deliberately brought up things that I wanted to learn about. Like I might say that I wondered how many cat breeds there were or what the most popular ice cream flavor was.

There were about a dozen people in the convenience store, talking and laughing like they all knew each other. It was like the whole tiny village was there at the same time, buying an overpriced loaf of bread or microwaving a bean burrito. It was probably the big thing for them, hanging out at the gas station convenience store. They probably stood around there all day, refilling a fountain soda and jabbering on in strange languages. They probably thought that was living high. It didn't look like there was anything else to do around there.

Ree followed me in, and the whole place got quiet for a minute. She had that copper-red hair and pale skin that got sunburned no matter how much sunscreen she tried to keep on it.

Everybody else looked Mexican or Native. Or at least partly, like me. Ree told me once that sometimes the locals thought whites were cops or something.

Harley followed Ree. Then Rex came in too, looking for the men's room. Ree had made Harley grab Rex's wallet out of his jeans while he slept in the van, then she took some money out of it. Rex didn't look mad, though. Either he hadn't noticed his money was missing yet or he didn't care.

Ree said we couldn't buy anything but Harley argued and she said, "Okay, fine. One small snack and one drink apiece. That's it." She wouldn't have given in to me like that. She handed me a ten-dollar bill, to pay for Harley's and my treats. When I came outside, I held my orange soda and bag of chips down at my side, so they wouldn't be very noticeable and maybe make her mad. She was standing in the parking lot, eating an apple and looking around, all happy, like we were at Disney Land or something instead of in this ugly, micro slum.

Ree just loved sad, pitiful places. She said it was how people were meant to live, in small groups, close to nature. I didn't see how anyone could live close to nature in the desert. Not for long, anyway. They'd die because there wasn't any water.

I also didn't get why we were going to Albuquerque, when Ree thought Roswell was way too big. Albuquerque was ten times the size of Roswell. I knew, because Ree had just made me look up Albuquerque and read about it out loud, as part of my school for the day. I'd reminded her that school was almost out for the summer but she said summer break didn't apply, here in the real world. That's what she always said but it didn't hurt to try anyway.

Ree noticed my bag of chips. She said, "Ha, Sayulita brand. They sell those at the jail commissary." I couldn't tell if she was trying to be friendly or if she was hinting that I should be in jail. You couldn't always tell with Ree.

She pointed her apple core at a small adobe house that was obviously abandoned. She said, "Now, that one looks old enough to be authentic. Those thick walls are what you need in the desert. They keep the inside cooler when it's hot outside and warmer when it's cold outside. They regulate the temperature just like a cave does." She said that every time she spotted an old adobe house. She acted like it was her big Hollywood-style dream to live in one. They were really just mud huts, when you thought about it. Well, clay huts. Same thing.

Ree and I tried to stay in an abandoned adobe house once, on some time free. But it was already occupied by a family of rattlesnakes, so we got to sleep in the van for a change.

She said, "See if you can look up that specific house. Then look up how to legally get ownership of an abandoned house, according to New Mexico law. Just see what you can find and write me a report."

"We're getting a house?" Ree always said only domestic livestock owned houses.

"No, but you might want one someday, Susie suburbs. So just do what I say."

Back in the van, I wrote down the name of the gas station and what I could see of the street names. I'd try to look up the house on Ree's phone. It was exciting to think of owning a house of my own someday, a home that nobody could make me leave. I wondered if you had to be a certain age to buy a house or if kids could buy houses too, if they had the money.

Rex and Harley came out and we got back on the road. Harley got to ride up front with Ree again, which wasn't fair. It hurt, knowing Ree had been hanging out with this kid after ditching me, her real kid. I couldn't tell if she really liked him best or if she was just acting like it, to get on Rex's good side. I worked on an E-Z crossword puzzle book that I found in the van. Ree made Harley spell easy words that she called out as she drove, words like van, sun and dog. She asked him, "Speaking of dogs, do you want your collar back on now?"

He nodded "yes," all eager, like he just couldn't wait to have a dog collar around his neck. Harley seemed like he would do anything to make Ree happy. Ree thought males were like dogs but she wasn't trying to be mean. She just thought it was the true male nature.

Harley barked a couple of times. Rex got that serious look on his face again but he didn't say anything.

I flung some of my chips at Rex. It was his punishment for just laying there looking stupid, I guess.

He smiled. Maybe he'd be all right, after all. It was too soon to know for sure. But somehow, I seemed to have activated him. "Redbone," he called, picking chips up off the floor of the van and eating them.

Ree put on an old song, "Come and Get Your Love," which turned out to be by a Native band called Redbone. Other Redbone songs came on after that. Rex told us what year each of the songs had been released and what was going on with the Redbone band at that time. I didn't really care about it. Once in a while, I'd throw something at him just to liven things up. A balled up pair of socks, an empty Kleenex box, my empty soda can. He didn't seem to care.

It got a little greener and bushier near Albuquerque. When we pulled into the city itself, there was lots of turquoise blue. There was turquoise blue trim on the buildings, turquoise blue lettering on the street signs, even turquoise blue parking lot stripes and license plates. It didn't go with the tan and sage desert landscape. It was kind of sickening, really. But it was nothing compared to the horrible purple walls in Rex's house.

#

Rex had a small, old, ugly house with a sagging porch roof. But after a few weeks there, I didn't really notice it anymore. Besides, any house was a whole lot better than no house to me. Luckily, only the main rooms were bright purple, the kitchen and living room. My bedroom walls were an okay cream color, though a little scuffed up, especially above the bed where Harley used to put his feet up on the wall, before I took the bed for myself.

It had just occurred to me that maybe I could clean the marks off the walls, so I was wiping them down with Fabuloso and water. I said, "If you put your feet on the walls anymore or even get on this bed with your shoes on, I'll spank you."

He looked confused for a minute, like he was trying to figure out if I was someone who had the authority to spank him or not. To stop his probably questioning me in his little dog head, I reached under the bed and pulled out the coffee can I kept my money in. I said, "I guess Harley doesn't want any more Walmart money," looking around the room like I was talking to somebody besides him.

That got him. We liked to walk over to Walmart and I'd usually give him a dollar or two to spend, to shut him up so I could look around in peace. "Okay, okay, I won't. I won't! Ruff-ruff!" he begged. He barely wore shoes anymore, anyway. He barely wore clothes at all, for that matter, since Ree had taught him that he was a dog.

When I got a chance, I added some fiery red to my room. Unlike the Albuquerque turquoise blue, I thought it went nicely with the soft desert colors outside my window. And I loved having a room that I'd decorated myself. That made it my home, somewhere I belonged instead of just another place where I was only passing through.

Well, what I saw from my bedroom window wasn't exactly the natural desert but it was still in desert colors. There was a gravel parking lot with patches of scruffy dried grass growing through it. That, and a long, one-story apartment building on the other side of the parking lot. The apartment building was in a complex of other buildings just like it. The buildings looked like giant mud bricks, with rectangles cut out for windows and doors. Red was also the color Bonnie Sue and I did my bedroom in, back in Roswell. It felt cozier to have red here too, a connection between here and there. That red was a brighter, sillier shade of red, though. This was chili pepper red, a more sad and grown-up color.

I had to share the room with Harley but he was okay, mostly. I pushed his dog bed under my real bed during the day. I'd bought fiery, chili pepper red bed sheets with some of my money from Lella, who paid me to help her. With five little kids, lots of migraine headaches and a husband who always came home drunk, she needed a lot of help. I stood on a kitchen chair, with some safety pins, finishing up on pinning a red sheet into place on the curtain rod.

"I'm gonna add white and blue, like the flag," Harley said.

"Oh no, you don't. This is my room, Bowzer. I say what goes."

"Ruff-ruff," he said.

"Ruff-ruff-*ruff*," I answered, climbing down from the chair, then standing back to admire my new makeshift curtains. I said, "Now, go put this chair back in the kitchen. Then you can grab a treat out of the jar."

He eagerly picked up the chair and hurried out of the room with it. "Slow down, you'll bang up the walls," I called after him. "And you better not take more than one treat."

Someone knocked on the door. I went after Harley, whispering, since the windows were open. I said, "Put your clothes on. And take off the collar."

He started to argue but I held up his dog treat jar as a bribe. Of course he didn't want to put on clothes because dogs don't wear clothes. I wished the whole dog game would end. Especially since here in town, there were a lot of nosy-rosies who could make trouble for us. That's what Lella said, that some people would never understand a dog game. We'd have CYFD at our door, Lella aid, and they were very close-minded. It wouldn't matter one bit to them that Harley actually liked being a dog.

I snuck a look out the window, next to the front door. It was only Lella. She said, "Hey there. Can you come over and help me for a while?"

"Okay," I said. "I'll be right over." She left and I sat down on the sofa for a minute, to get my mind ready for the big mess that I knew would be waiting for me over there.

I said to Harley, "Want to come with me or stay here?" Lella's kids were ages one to nine years old, so seven-year-old Harley fit right in.

"I want to come!" he said. I knew he would.

"Okay, but you better not act like a dog over there. The other kids will think you're a weirdo." I told him this all the time, just in case. He already knew it, though.

He made his pouty face but nodded.

The Montoyas lived in one of the apartments in the long ugly building across the parking lot. It was bigger than our house, with three bedrooms and two bathrooms, but it was still pretty small for seven people.

I knocked on the door and Lella yelled to come in. She said, "I'm gettin' one of my headaches. Can you just take over for a while?" She didn't look good at all. She was real sweaty too, though it was the beginning of October now and cool with the windows open.

"Okay," I said. In a way, I liked it better when Lella went out or stayed in her bedroom. I had to do all the work myself that way but I could just dive in and get to it without always having to work around however Lella wanted to do things. She also made me kind of nervous, and not just because she was an adult. She was always telling me too much of her business, like about how her husband didn't want to fuck her and how she thought he was cheating on her.

If you asked me, they didn't need to fuck anymore because they had too many kids as it was. And, I didn't say it to her but I thought it was really weird that she actually wanted to have sex with sneaky, drunk, pock marked face Juan. In fact, I was kind of amazed that he got the chance to cheat on her.

The whole idea of them having sex was supersonic gross. Lella was bigger than him but they both had great big Humpty-Dumpty middles, so I didn't know how it would even be possible for them to do it. If they tried, they'd probably just boing off each other and fly through the air in opposite directions, like if you slapped two balloons together. Then she went in her bedroom and shut the door and I felt bad for thinking mean stuff about her when she was sick.

I'd been helping Lella for a few weeks and Ree had made me study some babysitting sites for part of my school work. But they didn't cover a lot of the stuff I had to deal with at Lella's. For example, I figured out that the first thing to do when you went into a disorderly home was to check for danger. I added that part on myself, see. The babysitting sites did have some good tips, though. Like that you shouldn't leave anything around toddlers that was small enough to fit through a toilet paper roll, because they could choke on it.

With Lella in her bedroom, I got to work. Everybody looked okay, so I made a quick swoop through the living room and kitchen, picking up little toy soldiers, dice, coins, and other small things.

The oldest kid, Marco, who was the big boss of the other Montoya kids and Lella too, half the time, said, "Hey! What are you doing?"

I said, "Top secret. I'll tell you in a sec." Then I put a bottle of bleach back in its place, in the high up cabinet with the childproof latch. I snatched a lighter off the kitchen table, and a big plastic bag off the kitchen floor. It was probably a miracle that all of Lella's kids were even still alive. Unless there were more who had died from her sloppy ways, that she was too ashamed to admit to.

Next, I checked out each kid more closely, youngest to oldest. The baby, Marigold, needed a diaper change. I handled that. The twins, Monty and Monique, seemed okay, watching TV. Then there was Marisol, twirling in the middle of the room. She said, "I'm a ballerina."

I said, "Just stay off the bluffs," and laughed at how funny I was. I put Marco and Harley to work making peanut butter and jelly sandwiches, with bananas and potato chips. We'd have a super simple dinner, because there was a lot to do.

I'd have to finish cleaning up the place, which was a lot. The sink and countertop overflowed with dirty, smelly dishes, for one thing. The kids all needed baths. And a hill of dirty laundry was piled up by the front door.

After dinner, I grabbed Lella's jar of quarters and her laundry soap and got everybody together for the journey to the apartment complex laundry room. We'd have to stay there the whole time because Lella always worried that somebody would steal their clothes. I brought along a stack of picture books to read to the kids, and coloring books and crayons. I hoped it would be enough to keep them from running wild like they usually did.

Finally, a few hours later, the laundry was folded and put away, the apartment was clean, and all five Montoya kids were bathed and in bed. Harley had fallen asleep on the sofa opposite mine. I was tired but proud of myself for bringing order to the Montoya mess once again. I didn't want to ever have kids myself, though.

Lella always told me how tied down and trapped she was because of the kids, and her life did seem really hard and boring. Ree didn't seem to really like being a mother, either. Or she'd only liked it at first. She told me once that she'd named me Star because I had been her shining star, high above the wooden world. That was nice, even though she said it in past tense. I'd overheard Bonnie Sue tell Miss Annette that Ree had wanted to name me Desert Star but my dad had put his foot down because it was a stripper name. I thought it was pretty, though. I could have gone by Desi.

I'd only thought about ever being a mother myself after living with Harley and sort of feeling like I was his mother, sometimes. Ree and Rex kind of dumped him on me, then acted like Harly and I were just two kids playing together. As if a mature almost-twelve-year-old with a job would really even play at all, let alone want to play with a little seven-year-old. Or they'd act like Harley could really take care of himself and I just fixed his dinner and made sure he took his bath and everything because that was my idea of fun or something. Really, when you saw something in front of you that needed to be done, you'd most likely just do it, practically automatically.

Everybody was asleep and it didn't look like Lella was going to wake up and pay me, so I was thinking about just waking Harley up and going home. Then the front door flew open. It was Lella's husband.

Juan wasn't walking straight and his voice was slurry. He said, "Oh, what's this? A baby beauty queen, right here waiting for Papi to come home, eh?" I jumped up, ready to push past him like I did that other time he came home drunk and started it with me.

"Well, I have to go now," I said real loud, hoping to wake Lella, or at least Harley.

"Shhh. Not so fast, pretty girl," he said. He steered me over to the wall. "Look here," he said, one arm around me, the other at his zipper. "Don't be afraid of it."

I looked down. I would have shrieked with laughter if I wasn't too busy shaking, because I was terrified. He really did look like a balloon man and this was the stem, the part that would be tied into a knot and stick out on the end.

"Harley! Get up. Let's go!" I shouted.

That seemed to startle them both. Harley scrambled to his feet. He said, "What's wrong?"

I said, "Come on." I pushed past Juan and out the door.

Harley rushed out after me. "Want me to go back there and bite his ass?" he said.

That made me laugh, even with the bees buzzing crazy loud in my head. I said, "You're a good puppy dog, the best. You know that?"

Back home, Rex must have just come in because he was still in his security guard uniform. Ree stood at the sink, filleting the fish she'd caught earlier in the day.

Harley said, "We saw Juan's dick."

I said, "That's not funny. Don't make up nasty lies." *Oh god*. Now it would turn into a whole big thing and I'd have to worry about Juan catching up to me. Lella would probably hate me, too. And I could just forget about adding one more dime to my coffee can. Making my own money was the thing I was most proud of in the whole world, too.

Ree looked up from cleaning her fish. Rex looked at me, too. It was too much. I rushed into my bedroom, locked the door and flopped down on the bed, in the dark.

I heard low voices from the other room, then the front door opened and closed. I wanted to leave Albuquerque right away.

After a while, Harley knocked on the door. "Ruff-ruff?" he said. I got up and let him in.

"Mom said to tell you dinner's ready," he said, not looking at me.

"Mom?"

"Yeah, Ree. Mom. Ruff." I caught his gaze and he looked down again.

I knew he didn't mean to blabber. He was just a little kid and didn't know any better. I said,

"You're still a good dog. Come here." I scooted over and made room for him, then lay in the dark, petting his little dog head.

The fried fish was crispy and delicious. Ree's fish was baked instead, with only salt and pepper and a squeeze of lemon juice.

I said to Ree "Don't you think we've been in Albuquerque long enough? I think it's getting wooden now."

She was on to me, though. She said, "Males are starting to show interest, since you've started your period now. It would only be the same kind of stuff at the next place anyway, you know."

Rex came back in and sat down to eat. He didn't say anything. There was just the clatter of utensils on the plates.

#

Two days later, Harley and I came home from our schooling for the day, which was wandering around the Albuquerque Museum for two hours.

We'd just stepped into the house, when Lella knocked on the door. I didn't know how I missed seeing her on our way in. Had she been hiding out, waiting to pounce? I thought, *Oh god. Here it comes.* I didn't know what "it" would be, just that it probably wouldn't be good.

"Knock-knock!" she chirped, through the open window next to the door. She didn't sound mad.

I whispered to Harley, "Get the bat, guard dog." He crawled over to the closet where we kept our home security baseball bat. I fished the pocketknife out of my sock, opened it and stuck it into my back pocket, blade down. I put the chain lock on the door, then opened the door a crack. "Yeah?" I said.

"Hey there. Wanna come help me for a couple of hours?"

"Now?" Either she didn't find out that Juan tried something on me, or she planned to lure me into her apartment and behead me or something.

She said, "Yeah. If you can."

Whatever was coming, I decided I may as well get it over with. I said, "Um, okay. I'll be over in a sec."

After I was sure she was gone, I said, "Okay, good dog. Now tell me, the other night, after we were at Lella's and I went into our bedroom by myself, what all went on?"

"I don't know. Dad asked me what happened and I told him that man showed you his dick and you yelled and woke me up and I saw it, too. And then Dad left."

"What did Ree say?"

"Nothing. *Mom* just asked me if I wanted ketchup or ranch dressing with my fish."

"That's it?"

"Yes. Ruff-ruff. Can I have a treat?"

"Yeah, okay. Good dog." I opened the jar of Milk-bones and handed him one. I said, "Want to come with me to Lella's? Marco should be home from school in a while."

"Yes!"

"Remember, you can only be a dog at home. Right?"

"Ruff."

"Okay. Finish that dog treat first. And you know, seven is about the limit for boys to be dogs. Seven-and-a-half year olds usually start to think it's baby stuff."

He looked like he was thinking it over. I doubted Ree would even notice if Harley stopped being a dog now. She was always off fishing or trying to kill supper with a slingshot or picking plants in the desert. It was like she'd come home at night but her mind was more on getting her time free during the day. Ree didn't like cities.

My Life

I shut my pocketknife but kept it handy in my back pocket. You never knew. Especially since Lella had told me once about some girl she'd dragged out of Juan's car and beat up, a long time ago. She kind of scared me at the time, with how excited she seemed about it, telling me about each kick, punch and cuss word. She didn't say the girl's age.

But when we got there, Lella still just seemed like her usual self. I started washing dishes without saying anything. Staying busy kept my nerves steadier. Also, I was kind of mad because the place already looked like a tornado hit it again. I knew that if Lella didn't let her place get out of hand so fast, she wouldn't need so much help and my coffee can wouldn't be so full. But sometimes it made me mad anyway.

"Did Juan pay ya the other night?" she said.

Oh god, I thought. She's bringing up Juan. Here it comes. I said, "No." I focused on scrubbing the heck out of the cast iron skillet with a scrubby pad.

"How about a Coke?" she said. Oh, god. She offered me Cokes when she wanted to talk.

Lella seemed like she meant to be nice but her and Juan were both kooky, if you asked me. It was like they just didn't know what a kid was. Marco even bossed them around and he was only nine. And me, well they both seemed to think I was not really an eleven-year-old but really an extra young and extra short adult or something. They both made me nervous. I liked it better here when they were both gone.

Lella fixed two Cokes on ice and handed me one, without waiting for my answer on if I wanted it or not. Then she started talking, fast, like she just couldn't wait one more second to get back on her favorite topic, which was what Juan did to her this time.

She said, "Oh, Star. Well, I'm sure you already know about this, since you seen him before I did. I says to him, 'If you'd come home to your family after work instead of going to the bar, you wouldn't be getting in no bar fights, would ya?'"

Lella liked to talk about how she'd put Juan in his place. She didn't seem to notice that he'd always just go do the same things again anyway.

"He don't know who jumped him, just that it was two guys in the parking lot. Even I felt sorry for him, if you can believe that. He had a busted nose, two black eyes and a tooth knocked out. In the end they didn't even take his wallet. Can you believe that? I bet even they felt sorry for him after the way they worked him over."

"Yeah. I mean, no." I couldn't keep up with her. But I didn't remember Juan being beat up.

Maybe he went back out after Harley and I left. Maybe he went for a hot air balloon ride, with his icky self as the hot air balloon and his icky stem flopping in the breeze.

Juan came out of their bedroom then. I didn't know he was home. His eyes got big when he saw me. His eyes had purple bruising all around them. He stepped back into the bedroom and closed the door.

Lella said, "Yeah, he had to take a couple of days off work."

Harley was on the living room floor, fitting Lego blocks together. I'd already warned him that he better keep his snout shut.

When we got home, it was like a re-play of that other night. Rex was standing there in his security guard uniform, like he'd just walked in the door. Ree was at the sink, only this time she was messing with some wild sage and other stuff she'd gathered in the desert that day.

Rex said, "Where were you two at?"

It was weird, how Rex had turned into a regular husband and dad type guy, instead of a goof ball who only talked when it was about the Redbone band. I said, "Helping Lella."

"Did everything go okay?"

"Yeah."

He said, "Any more trouble over there, you let me know." He kind of smiled and nodded, like he was proud of himself. Then I knew it for sure. He was the one who beat Juan up.

My breath caught in my throat. A grown man beat up another grown man for trying something on me. I was highly honored but also mortified. I couldn't believe it. The thought popped up in my mind that if Harley was going to call Ree "Mom," maybe I could call Rex "Dad." But then even thinking that embarrassed me, too. I said, "Eh, all the trouble's over here," and flung a handful of dog treats at Rex.

#

The pistachios were ready to harvest in Alamogordo. They were late this year, Ree said. She said we'd go there to help out and make a few bucks. We'd been in Alamogordo on time free one year when the pistachios ripened. The farmer flooded the trees with water to swell the pistachios. Then you could hear the pistachio shells cracking open on the trees. It sounded like popcorn popping, *pop-pop-pop*.

Alamogordo was three hours away, too far to drive back and forth every day.

"How long would we be gone?" I said, looking up from my project. I'd just bought a sewing machine with some of my money from Lella and was excited about taking it out of the box. I was setting it up at the kitchen table, along with fabric to make throw pillows for my bed. The fabrics were coordinated prints that all included the chili pepper red color. I'd already cut the fabric into squares. When the pillows were finished, I planned to line them up along my bedroom wall, down the length of my twin bed, to make it look like a daybed. I loved making my little space look settled and homey. I loved it more than anything.

Ree picked up the edge of a large red and brown batik fabric square and looked it over, shaking her head, disappointed in me again. To Ree, I was domestic livestock.

She said, "We'll come back when we're finished. That's when."

I said, "I don't want to go. I'm in the middle of making these pillows and Lella's baby is due any day now. I promised to help her." I also had a new friend, Juno, whose family had moved in next door to Lella. When you took a trip with Ree, there was a good chance you wouldn't be coming back at all. I didn't want to be ripped out of the life I'd settled into and plopped down somewhere new again.

Ree went to the fridge for a THC gummy, then held the jar out to me. Acting like I was her adult pal, just like Lella did.

"No, thanks. I have to be able to sew these seams straight," I said, which Ree thought was hysterical, for some reason.

"I'll go with you, Mom," Harley said.

Ree packed some tobacco into her pipe and lit it. Finally, she said, "Nah, that's all right. You two can stay here with Tyrannosaurus Rex."

Tyrannosaurus Rex. Ree started calling her guys' names when things were going wooden.

#

Ree drove away in our old van by herself. The week after that, the Albuquerque balloon festival started. Me, Harley and Rex got up extra early and put on our jackets, then ate oatmeal with raisins at the picnic table on our back patio. Dozens of brightly colored hot air balloons floated through the chilly morning sky. It was magical. That was the only word for it. Rex and Harley both said they'd go up in one right now, if they had the money. But I said no way, uh-uh, never.

Later in the day, it warmed up outside. Harley and I kept Rex company while he cooked burgers on the grill. As the burgers hit the buns, and Rex insisted we had to have green chile on them because that's the way it was done in New Mexico, I suddenly realized that I was having lunch with my family. I felt like we had become a real, normal family, even when Ree wasn't there.

But Ree wasn't forgotten for long. Rex had brought her up a lot in the past few days since she'd been gone. Between bites of his burger, he said, "Here, you try calling her. She's not answering me." He dialed Ree's number and put the phone on speaker. It went to voice mail. "Leave a message," he said.

I did, but I doubted it would make any difference. Rex had already called the pistachio farms. He kept asking me questions about Ree, like if she'd ever just taken off before.

I didn't tell him anything, though. Ree wouldn't like it. I thought about myself, about what would be the best thing to say, if she didn't come back soon, so I could maybe stay here anyway. So much for this being my family. It had seemed like it for a minute there, that was all.

"Maybe I should call the police," he said.

The police. God, no. I said, "That would make her super mad. Ree doesn't like the cops. And they might take me away, which would make her super mad. And then, who would watch Harley when you're at work?"

It seemed like he was listening to me, so I continued. "I know, let's call the jails and the hospitals. But no cops." There. That should keep him busy for a while.

I made a big show of helping Harley fix his plate, asking him how many spoonfuls of baked beans he wanted, and how about some of that apple sauce? It was a reminder to Rex of why he should want to keep me around.

As if things weren't bad enough, just then Juan came around back. He took his cap off and held it in front of him when he saw Rex. He said, "Hello, sir. Can Star come over? Lella's gone into labor." The purple bruising around his eyes was a weird greenish yellow color now.

Juan was acting like Rex was his boss. He was probably afraid of getting his butt whooped again for being a pervert.

Rex just nodded, then went back to eating, like Juan was barely even there.

I said, "Okay, I'll be right there." I avoided looking at Juan, who scampered off right away anyhow.

I went in the house to put my supper in the fridge and grab a couple of books.

Rex said, "Harley, you go with her."

Ever since the thing with Juan, Rex had assigned Harley as my protector. Harley took it seriously, too. Like, he'd walk on the side closest to the street and he'd insist on going through doorways first, explaining to me why it was the man's job. Rex must have told him all that. Sometimes Harley was adorable.

When we got to the Montoya's place, Lella was doubled over in pain. Her kids were gathered around her, quiet for a change. Even the baby looked serious, on Marisol's hip.

Juan helped Lella out the door. Then I had the usual Montoya disaster to deal with. I had Marco and Harley make peanut butter and jelly sandwiches, while I did my usual sweep for dangerous items, then looked each kid over, youngest to oldest. Luckily, the laundry was already washed and folded, on the kitchen table. I'd just have to put it away this time.

#

Rex came over at about ten p.m., after the Montoya kids were in bed. He said, "A nurse from the hospital called. You'll have to spend the night." He'd brought pajamas for me and Harley and our toothbrushes.

Rex lay down on one of the sofas. He said, "I called the hospitals and jails between here and Alamogordo. Nobody's seen Ree." He looked very worried and sad and it made me mad. Rex was so good. He didn't deserve this. It hit home, how Ree hurt people, when I saw her do it to someone else. Why couldn't she at least just return a phone call?

It seemed like Rex planned to spend the night here, too. So I said, "I'm sure you could sleep in Juan and Lella's room, if you want."

So he went in there, and I went to the closet to get blankets for me and Harley. I had too much on my mind to concentrate on reading the books I'd brought or even on doing a word search. I lay there in the dark, trying to figure out my next move. Ree probably wasn't coming back soon. Otherwise, why would she be hiding out from us in the first place.

I wanted to stay here, where I'd put in four hard months setting up my new life. Now I had my room fixed up, my job and my new friend, Juno. Not to mention a sort-of family, Rex and Harley. I felt successful and happy and nobody bothered me, ever since Rex beat up Juan. The only thing wrong was Ree. Once in a while, I'd feel a thump in my chest and have the awful thought that Ree might be dead. But I couldn't do anything about it but just feel terrible and get on with things anyway.

But what if Rex wouldn't keep me, what then? Maybe then I could stay with Lella. It sounded awful, though. She had a lot of kids. I'd probably never get a break.

I didn't know Juno that well yet, and had only met her mom once. So I really doubted I could live there. Then there was Bonnie Sue and my dad. But Ree always came back for me, sooner or later, and then I'd make Bonnie Sue cry all over again. I still saw that look on her face sometimes when I drifted off to sleep. Ree might have wanted to name me Desert Star but she should have named me Dust Devil because I just seemed to skip all around the desert, with a big mess swirling around me everywhere I went.

I woke to daylight and the sound of little Marigold crying. I went to get her and noticed that Lella's bedroom door was open. Rex had already left. Harley was still asleep on the other couch.

I changed the baby and brought her into the kitchen for a bottle. The door opened just then. Lella came in. She was alone. I didn't know how she got home or why the new baby wasn't with her. It seemed wrong to ask, so I just said, "Hi."

"Hey there. Can you help me get to bed, and stay with the kids for a while?"

I said, "Okay." I really wanted to go home, but I let her put her arm around my neck and I helped her walk to the bedroom. Then I brought her some water so she could take the pills the doctor sent her home with.

The rest of the kids started waking up. I turned cartoons on with the sound low and fixed each one a bowl of cereal as they came out.

After everybody was fed and dressed, I got out the coloring books, the Play Doh and the puzzles, and set them all up at the kitchen table. The older kids took their seats and I sat on a blanket on the floor with baby Marigold and some of her toys.

I worried that the new baby had died. Which reminded me that Ree might have died, too. I grabbed a coloring book and a couple of crayons and started coloring in a big teddy bear, just to have something nicer to think about than who might have died.

Someone knocked on the door. It was a heavy lady with a lot of makeup and jewelry. She kind of pushed her way in, while she talked.

Marco said, "Aunt Helena!"

I was really glad he said that, because otherwise I'd just let a strange woman push her way into the apartment.

The woman hugged him, then sat at the table and explained that she was going to take them all to Texas, where they would live with her, in her big house. She said she had a built-in swimming pool and a yellow labrador retriever named Rubio. She looked too old to be Lella's sister. I wondered if she was really Lella's aunt.

Marco said, "Is my mom coming, too?"

"Of course she is," Aunt Helena said.

"Is my dad coming, too?" Marco said, suspicious, wise.

"Oh, no, honey. He has to stay here and… work."

Marco said, "Is the new baby coming to Texas?"

"No, honey. You see, your mom already has all of you, so the new baby went to a different mommy and daddy. They're really nice and so very happy because they couldn't have any children of their own."

"Oh." Marco seemed to be seriously thinking over all of this unexpected news. The other kids looked up from their table activities, looking to Marco for guidance. I didn't like it when they did that. I was the one in charge. They should look to me.

Marco said. "Well, when are we going?"

"In a couple of days, honey, or maybe even a week. We have to wait until your mom gets a good, long rest and feels all better."

I wished I could go to Aunt Helena's big house in Texas with the swimming pool and the big dog too. But she said, "I'll take it from here, honey. You and your brother can go on home now."

She pulled two twenty-dollar bills from her purse and handed them to me. She smelled like expensive flowers.

Lella had told me that she'd be coming home with the new baby and that I was supposed to help her with it a lot, for at least the first couple of weeks. I was even supposed to bring Juno over to meet Lella, in case she needed more help than just me. I didn't know why everything had suddenly changed.

But Harley and I went home. And before long, there was a new family in the Montoya's apartment, an old couple with two old daughters, like college age, at least.

#

Rex came home from work one evening as usual, a few days before Christmas. I was trying hard to be too useful to get rid of, so I had dinner on the stove. Tonight it was macaroni and cheese from a box, with canned tuna and frozen peas mixed in.

At the table, he said, "We've got to talk." That wasn't a sentence I wanted to hear.

He said, "All right now, we'll wait until the start of the summer for your mother to come back to us."

That was a long way off, like five months away. I could breathe again.

He started eating again and I thought that was all he had to say. "Okay," I said, and I started eating again, too.

Then he said, "But."

Oh god. But. Here it comes.

He wiped his mouth with the paper towel I'd placed so neatly under his silverware. "This..." He waved his fork at me and Harley, "Has to stop."

What has to stop? I was afraid of saying the wrong thing and throwing my whole life off the rails. So I just waited, heart pounding.

He said, "You kids need to be in school. In *real* school. I signed you both up. You'll start after the Christmas break."

"But Rex!" I started.

"But Dad!" Harley said.

"That's it. It's done."

He finished his dinner in a couple more bites, put his dishes in the sink, and went into his bedroom.

Harley and I sat there, sadly shaking our heads.

Finally, just to break the weird head shaking spell, I said, "You can't act like a dog at school, you know. Everyone will think you're a weirdo."

He said, "I don't care. I hardly even do that dog stuff anymore, anyhow. I'm too old for it."

Huh. Come to think of it, I hadn't seen him do the dog stuff for a while. It's like it quietly slipped away when Ree did.

#

Juno and I got off the school bus and trudged through a light blanket of snow. We went straight to my house, as usual. Then I grabbed a pack of saltines out of the cabinet and lit my lemon-scented jar candle. I'd gotten into the habit of buying candles and lighting them. It made me feel grown-up and it brightened the grayness of winter.

"Want some tea?" I said. That was another mature thing Juno and I had started doing, drinking hot tea. We were in the sixth grade, middle school, which made us feel a bit adult. In fact, we even called ourselves "young adults."

We got situated at the kitchen table to do our homework, starting with the career exploration assignment that we both had to do.

"Did you get any closer to deciding what you want to do when you're older?" I said. I wanted to be an interior decorator. Or rather, an interior designer, which sounded more serious, I thought.

"Mm-hmm."

"Well, what?"

Juno said, "A stripper, duh." She started dancing around all crazy in her chair.

"Ha-ha! I dare you to write that on your paper."

"No. But really, I do know something that's… mmm. I have a big, big secret."

"What? What? What?" I stirred three spoonfuls of sugar into my tea, then took a careful sip.

"Well, Cyrus told me. I mean, he showed me. But I'm not supposed to say anything. It would blow. Your. Mind."

Cyrus, Juno's brother, was sixteen and a stoner. After I finally admitted I'd never kissed a guy before, she made Cyrus teach me to French kiss, so I wouldn't feel stupid when my time came for real. Juno was a super good friend like that, always looking out for you.

I said, "What, what, chicken butt?" Great best friend or not, Juno was getting too much mileage out of trying to make me beg.

"Well, okay. But I mean it, you have to swear not to tell a soul. You can never, ever tell Cyrus I told you, either."

"Okay. I swear." I crossed my heart.

"All right. I know where there's a… Oh, I can't even say it."

"What, what, what, what, what?" She was driving me crazy.

"I know. I'll show you. That way, I'm not exactly telling. But remember, you swore." She put her coat back on, and so did I.

I left the door unlocked for Harley and followed Juno down the street. We walked in the direction away from the river. I felt my mood lift, being out and about in the world. The cold was energizing, since I was warm enough, in my coat, and with my scarf and gloves.

Finally, Juno turned to the driveway of an old house, with empty lots on either side of it. It didn't look like anybody had lived here for some time. The windows were boarded up. I said, "Juno?" but she shushed me.

I pulled my pocketknife out of my sock, opened it and gripped its handle, inside my coat pocket.

I followed her around back, to a small yard and a shed that was in as bad of shape as the house. Juno put her finger up to her lips, signaling me to stay quiet, then peeked in the shed's one window that wasn't boarded up. I followed her into the shed. The door's creaking giving me chills.

Inside, my gaze followed where she pointed, which was at a woman, who was sleeping on the ground. But no, she wasn't asleep.

She was dead.

She was very dead and kind of mummified. She had long black hair. Her eyes were closed and her skin looked leathery. The clothes were grimy and too big for the body, jeans and a man's shirt, blue flannel plaid with long sleeves.

"Oh my god, oh my god ohmygod." It was all I could think to say.

Then I was out the door, moving as fast as I could without slipping on the snow. I didn't stop until I was halfway down the block.

That's where Juno caught up with me.

"Told you," she said, in tone like she was quite satisfied with herself.

"I don't know what to say," I said, or tried to say, since my teeth were kind of chattering.

"That's good. Don't say anything. Remember, you---"

"Yeah, I know, I know. I promised. But... Why did I have to promise?"

We walked at a fast clip now, led by me. I wanted nothing more than to keep putting distance between myself that dead body. My brain bees buzzed like crazy, now that they'd had a chance to get over the shock enough to even buzz at all.

A while later, we passed a taco stand. Juno said, "Hold on." she went towards the ordering window.

I said, "Nah, I'm going home. Harley will be there soon." It was a lie and she knew it. Harley was eight now but he seemed older, especially now that he was in school, for some reason. He could stay home alone.

Juno said, "I'll be there in a few." I didn't know how she could eat right then. The girl was tough as nails. Or something.

Back home, I felt sort of frozen. It was a strange unreality feeling and I didn't like it at all. I thought about just not answering the door when Juno came back. I could just get rid of her and her horrifying secret.

My notebook was still open on the table, with the homework questions the teacher had made us copy. It seemed like it was from a long time ago, not just a half hour ago. It said:

Use the *Occupational Outlook Handbook* online to answer the following questions:

1. List your top three career choices: first choice, second choice, then third choice.

2. For each career chosen above, list the pay range.

3. For each career chosen above, list the education required.

4. For each career chosen above, list the projected job growth rate.

I pictured Ree, lying dead in an old shed somewhere, with her long, coppery hair the same as always but her pale skin gone leathery. The words I'd copied in my notebook swam around on the page.

#

The reason we couldn't report the dead body was supposedly because Cyrus and his friend had found it when they broke into the house and the shed, looking for stuff to steal. And they had taken a couple of things, a shovel and some tools. That was what Juno said. It seemed pretty stupid to me, though. I mean, why couldn't they just say they'd overheard some people talking about the dead body somewhere? Or they could even call it in anonymously. I really doubted that old house and shed had much left that was worth taking. Who would really care anyway, especially when you compared it with a dead body? It seemed stupid to me. I wondered if I could get in trouble for knowing something like that and not reporting it.

I didn't like thinking about it. Even though I tried to block it out, it weighed on me heavily. In the back of my mind, I felt like I would tell. But just not yet.

I especially tried to put it out of my mind today, because it was my birthday. Juno had brought over a Hostess cupcake with a candle in it. She lit it and told me to make a wish.

I wished the dark secret about the poor dead woman in the shed would be over. I wished Ree would come home to stay, or at the very least, call. I wished I didn't have to go to school. Well, I kind of was starting to like school but it was still for too many hours a day and there were too many people there.

Oh, I also wished more than anything that Reeve Salazar liked me back. Juno and I had many talks about how to let him know I liked him. But her ideas were too risky, if he didn't like me, too. The trick was to figure out how to let him know, in a way that would seem like I didn't mean it or something, if he didn't like me back. What was needed was a good hint.

"Hurry up," Juno said, so I blew out the candle.

Then she said, "Okay. Are you ready for your present now?"

I said, "Sure." I was pretty much always ready for a present.

"Close your eyes, then. And don't peek or you don't get it!"

I did what Juno said, as usual.

I heard the door open and felt a rush of cold air from outside.

Juno said, "Okay. Now you can open your eyes."

I opened my eyes, then shrieked and ran to hide in the bathroom. I heard laughter behind me. Laughter from Juno. And Reeve Salazar.

I brushed my hair and my teeth, while I was hiding out. They kept knocking on the bathroom door. I finally unlocked it and then they pulled me back down the hall to the living room.

"Birthday kiss!" Juno ordered. Reeve Salazar, the guy of my dreams, obeyed. I was glad I'd just brushed my teeth and glad Juno had made her brother give me that kissing lesson. The most important rules were to brush your teeth first, and to swallow your spit. She was the best friend I ever had. Aside from including me in that horrifying secret.

Harley came home. He puffed up all stern, like he was the man of the house, when he saw me sitting on Reeve Salazar's lap. It was so cute.

I made sure Juno and Reeve were gone way before the time Rex would be home. Having company over when he wasn't home, especially when one of them was a boy, didn't seem like a good idea. I had to be super careful so he wouldn't decide I was too much trouble to keep around.

Rex had told me he'd make my birthday dinner. He came home with a pack of hot dogs and buns and all the toppings, like shredded cheese, a can of chili and an onion. It was perfect. Then we had storebought chocolate cake with ice cream and he gave me a $50 gift Walmart gift certificate.

Later, in our bedroom, Harley gave me a pack of Marlboro cigarettes. I thought about lecturing him, since he's just a little kid and everything. But I just couldn't do it, when he seemed so proud of managing to get me something so forbidden and grown up. It was a pretty great birthday.

The next day, after Juno and I got home from school, but before Harley got home, there was a knock at the door. I peeked out the curtain and couldn't believe it. It was Ree.

She'd come home at last. As I opened the door, she called, *Yip, yip. Ruh-ray-ooo!*

Juno looked at me like what the hell is wrong with her?

I ignored the animal sounds and introduced them. Then Juno seemed to get it that my mother coming home was a big deal, and she left.

Ree and I didn't really ever hug and that kind of stuff. Instead, Ree said, "Here," and handed me a big bag of pistachios.

It kind of made me mad. Was it supposed to be a joke? Saying she was going to help with the pistachio harvest, then not even calling for over four months. And having the nerve to bring me a bag of pistachios when she finally did come back.

Maybe it wasn't supposed to be a joke, though. Ree didn't always think like other people. She went to the kitchen and got a glass of ice water.

I had to sit down because I felt dizzy, like my brain bees had given up on buzzing and just decided to drain the honey out of my head instead. I started to laugh at that because it was so stupid. Ree thought I was smiling at her or something. She smiled back, which made me mad again, for some reason.

"So, you're back," I said.

"I've come back to get you. And we need to get going," she said, looking at the time on her phone.

Yeah, she wanted me to sneak away from Rex and Harley now too, just leaving them to worry about if we were both dead in a shed this time. "I have a life going on here, you know!" I shouted.

Ree looked surprised, like she'd never even considered that before.

She sat there looking at me and taking sips of her water. Finally, she said, "Well, you decide what you want to do. I'll be back later. Happy birthday, by the way. In case you didn't know, that was the best day of my life. Well, not the birth. That hurt a lot. After that, I mean. That was the best day of my life."

I wondered if she was trying to make me feel guilty or something. I wondered if she knew that my birthday was actually yesterday.

Before I could think of what to say, she was gone again.

I didn't know what to do but I felt crazed right then. I grabbed a THC gummy out of the fridge for starters, to calm my mind. Then I thought, what the heck, and grabbed one of Rex's beers out of the fridge, too.

I started cooking and cleaning, back and forth between taking sips of beer to putting frozen pizzas in the oven to sweeping the floor to cutting up apple slices to rinsing out the kitchen trash can to setting the table to clearing off the coffee table. I kept moving.

Harley came home. A while after that, Rex came home. We sat down to eat the pizza.

Ree came back. I was surprised. But I guess she didn't care enough about Rex and Harley to go too awful much out of her way to avoid seeing them. They had worried and suffered so much when she went missing.

Rex told me to fix her a plate. I knew she wouldn't eat the pizza so I gave her a plate with a whole apple and some of her stupid pistachios on it.

Rex and Harley ate silently. It seemed like they were both practically holding their breath, waiting to see if Ree was back to stay. The hope on their faces made me want to cry.

It was too much. I left the table without finishing my dinner. I locked my bedroom door and lay on my pretty chili pepper red bed with all the cozy throw pillows I'd made.

Rex knocked on my bedroom door. He just said, "You have to go with your mother."

#

We didn't talk on the drive out of Albuquerque. My mind went back and forth between grieving the life and almost-family I'd just lost and being super mad about it. I didn't feel like talking to Ree.

Three hours later, we were in Alamogordo, where Ree had moved in with some old guy named Milo, behind our backs. We pulled right up to his front door. It was dark out but I could see that the place looked like a motel court, with old one-story buildings around a circular parking lot, and a built-in swimming pool in the center. It said "Apartments" on the sign, though.

Ree didn't make any sense. It seemed like she used men, sort of anyway, but then she didn't like the ones with money. She said, they weren't "real," whatever that was supposed to mean.

She only accepted Ree-jects. I almost said it out loud but she might think it was funny. The last thing I was in the mood to do was joke around with her.

Milo's apartment only had one bedroom, so I guessed I'd have to sleep on the couch. He had a fluffy orange cat, at least. I'd only get that one teeny-tiny piece of the dream life I carried around in my mind, a cat that wasn't even mine.

Milo got up from the couch, where he was watching *Hoarders* on TV. He said, "Well hello there, Star. We are so glad you're here." His eyes crinkled in the corners like he meant his smile.

The bees in my mind quieted down. He asked Ree, "Can I carry anything in for this young lady?"

Ree said there was another bag of my clothes in the van. Milo went out into the frosty night to get it.

When he came back, he said, "Now, how about a pizza?" I almost felt happy for a while, after I realized he was ordering delicious restaurant pizza on his phone, not just sticking a frozen grocery store pizza in the oven.

After he got off the phone, he said, "Okay, I've already spoken to the manager here about a larger apartment and she's put us on the waiting list. But we still have to wait until one becomes available. I wanted to wait to ask you, in the meantime, would you rather sleep on the couch or in the dining area? The couch is more comfortable. But we could put a bed sheet up across the dining alcove and then you'd have your own little area there. We could move the dinette set into the living room. But then you'd have to sleep in a sleeping bag.

"I'd rather have the dining area," I said, without even having to think about it. I wanted that curtain.

"All right, then. I'll get on it right after supper."

Milo seemed super nice so far. He weirdly reminded me of Bonnie Sue. He even looked kind of like her, like he could be her dad or something. And, after all, none of this was his fault, most likely.

Milo looked at his phone. He said, "Well, I better get going. The pizza place closes soon." He went to pick up our order. I got up off the floor and sat on the couch. The cat, whose name was Blaze, jumped up onto my lap and lay down across it.

Ree called from the kitchen, "Do you want a gummy?"

I said no. Not no thanks, just no. I didn't want the dizzy, unsure feeling gummies gave me and I didn't want the type of mom who asked me if I wanted a gummy. Did she think we were Selena and Madison from Roswell, or what? Gretel and her evil stepmother was more like it. I turned back to the TV show, petting warm, fluffy Blaze while he purred. I decided to call him Kirk, short for Albuquerque.

#

The next morning, Ree and Milo left early and I ate the rest of the wonderful leftover pepperoni pizza for breakfast. Pizza and the cat were the only two small bright spots in my ruined life so far. The pool would be a third small bright spot, if we were still here in the summertime. A swimming pool was included in my dream life, though I'd meant a swimming pool of my own.

There was a note on the coffee table, on top of two old books and a twenty-dollar bill. The note said:

1 Read three chapters each of Plants and Animals of Alamogordo and The History of

Alamagordo

2 Go to the grocery store. Buy: lettuce, tomato, carrots, radishes, zucchini, apple.

3 Make three salads with the above for dinner.

Ree had drawn a map to the grocery store. I took my shower and thought about writing Ree a list back, starting with don't disappear and don't uproot my life when you don't even have a good reason to.

I took my shower and thought about calling Bonnie Sue. I could just leave without a word and let Ree worry about if I was dead or alive. See how she liked it. There was no phone here, though.

The grocery store took me a long time. I kept putting things in the cart, then putting them back where I got them, then putting them back in the cart again. What kind of lettuce should I get? How many tomatoes? A couple of apples or a whole bag of them? I also had to make sure I didn't go over twenty dollars.

I was almost home with my bag of groceries when a boy who looked about my age opened the apartment door next to ours. He yelled, "Hey, want to fuck?"

I swooped down and grabbed my pocketknife out of my sock and hurried to Milo's place. After I'd opened the door, I shouted, "Go fuck your mom!" Then I went inside real quick and locked the door.

I was only a tiny bit scared, really. Boys were nowhere near as scary as girls. They usually only said dirty or stupid things if they liked you and wanted you to pay attention to them. Otherwise, they'd most likely just ignore you. Girls were the ones who would want to fight you. But I locked the deadbolt too, just in case.

The boy started knocking on the door. "Just a kiss, then!" he yelled. A different voice said, "He's sorry. Come hang out." I couldn't tell if that voice was from a boy or a girl. Then one of them opened the mail slot in the door and wiggled their fingers through it. The boy said, "Can I have a sandwich, at least?" They howled, like that was the funniest thing in the world.

I found some duct tape and taped the mail slot shut. After a few more knocks and comments, they went away. I wondered why they weren't in school.

I started making salads in three small bowls. Then I switched to three dinner plates. Then I gave up and just made it all in one big bowl. The problem was, I didn't know if the salads were supposed to be the main meal or just side dishes, so I didn't know how big the servings should be. Kirk jumped up on the table and lay across the cutting board. I opened a can of tuna and shared it with him.

My schoolwork only took about an hour, since I didn't read it all. Reading about Alamogordo bored me. But on the inside of the cover of one of the books, it said, "To Millward, All my Love, Mother." Milo's real name was Millward? It cracked me up. Who would name their kid Millward? It sounded like Squidward, from *SpongeBob SquarePants*. Of course, Millward Milo was so old that it could have been a stylish name way back then, like Roman or Grayson were today. It was hard to say.

There was no more noise from the stupid boy next door, which was a bit disappointing. I got an idea when I went to the bathroom. I grabbed a bar of soap, a tube of toothpaste and a deodorant stick, then tiptoed next door. I slipped them through the mail slot and ran back home. See how the dirty, stinky boy liked some nice personal hygiene products.

I waited and waited to see what the reaction would be. It stayed quiet though, so I guessed those two had gone somewhere. I turned on Judge Judy because I couldn't find anything better on TV. I didn't really like her, though. She was too mean and I'd feel sorry for the people she yelled at.

#

We were only there for about a week before Ree decided she had to get away from Micro Milo. He was a regular sized man so I didn't know what she meant by that. I didn't want to know, either. Regardless, according to Ree, things had gotten too wooden to stay.

Milo came home early from work, just as we were pulling out in Ree's van. He got out of his car and put his hand up, like he was asking Ree to stop so he could say something to her.

He had a big smile on his face. He didn't know we were leaving him. Ree laid on the horn, like she was trying to shock him into backing away from the van.

She finished backing out and we drove off. I watched him in the side mirror, standing there. His smile dropped into confusion as we rode out of his life.

Good-bye, Micro Milo, I thought. Good-bye Kirk, the beautiful, fluffy cat that was almost mine. Good-bye, dirty, stinky neighbor boy, whatever your name is. Enjoy the personal hygiene products.

#

We rode into Taos a couple of months after my fourteenth birthday. The first thing I noticed was that the fences were different. They were made from skinny, vertical tree limbs that still had the bark on them, instead of the regular fence boards, or the metal chain link fences like Bonnie Sue and Big Mom-Mom had.

From the school assignment Ree made me do, I'd also learned about the dark sky laws, where homeowners and business owners in Taos were strictly limited on how bright their outdoor lights could shine. Taos was a different kind of place, more in tune with nature. Ree liked that kind of stuff. It was also a very small town. If you didn't count tourists, the population here was only like 6,500. Alamogordo was 32,000. Roswell was close to 50,000 and Albuquerque, 575,000. So, if there was anywhere decent that Ree might settle down for good, Taos was a good bet.

We were on our way to stay with some guy Ree met from her last man-call dance, in a campground we'd been staying at on some time free. I hadn't met this guy yet but I didn't expect much, partly because he was the kind of guy who would go to a man-call dance.

The thing about Ree was she went into heat, the same as a female coyote or fox would. Or she thought she did anyway, which is why she thought her mating ritual was normal. She thought domestic livestock women were just too dumbed down by the domestic lifestyle to be in touch with their true natures. The domestic livestock stuff made sense, in a way. Take feral swine, for example. They had to fend for themselves to survive, which mad them a hundred times sharper than the dim and drowsy penned up pigs that spent their lives stupidly sitting around, waiting for food. It's just the way it was.

But the guys who answered the man-call dances weren't confused, see, and they didn't go by any mating season, any more than female domestic livestock humans did. They were just nasty. Ever since I got a womanly shape, I had to find somewhere to hide out whenever Ree started swaying.

But the main reason I didn't expect much from this guy wasn't because of all that. It was because his name was Toe. Ree could call me an uppity Ursula all she wanted, I still doubted that anybody who went by the name Toe could be that great.

I was reading *Interior Design Basics* on Ree's phone and trying to pretend I had a different life. Reading in a moving vehicle got tiring, though. Ree didn't consider interior design a school-worthy subject but it was a free download so I read it anyway. Besides, I didn't consider Ree to be an expert on worthiness.

But the home décor guides would hold my interest better if I had a place to decorate. Reading about things like how you could position a striped rug width-wise across a narrow room to make the room look wider was pretty boring when you didn't actually have a narrow room. Or any other room, either. I couldn't even decorate the interior of the van. Ree wouldn't let me, though it would be more cozy with some matching throw blankets and pillows, at least. And those were things we'd use all the time, so they wouldn't be wasting space.

The next section of the guide said to include a humorous or whimsical element in each room to avoid spaces that seemed to take themselves too seriously. One picture showed an ottoman that was shaped like a mushroom, in somebody's fancy living room. Another picture had a tiny, dollhouse-sized table and chair set, placed in the middle of a real dining table set. The miniature set was an exact copy of the full-sized table and chairs.

I thought of one of Ree's boyfriends, the one before the last one. His name was Chad, in Los Alamos. I knew things were going wooden when Ree started calling him Unclad Chad. It was only the truth, though, since Chad was a nudist for real, or a "naturist," as he called himself. Ree didn't care, except when she thought he was thinking about me when he got semi-hard. I never figured out how she decided on this, since I'd never caught him looking at me weird and he'd never even said anything weird to me. No perv vibe at all. But when Ree decided he was thinking nasty about me, she'd flick his thing with her middle finger and thumb. Or she'd slap it with the flyswatter or a spoon or the TV remote, or whatever else was nearby. Chad would yelp. He'd screech about how he didn't do anything wrong. It was pretty funny, in a fucked up way.

I didn't really miss him, though. He was okay but not one of my favorites. He was always blabbing on about ethical this and sustainable that. He was in his own naked goody-goody world. Also, we didn't eat our meals at the kitchen table there but just fixed our plates from the food on the stovetop. Then we'd eat in the living room, in front of the TV. Because of the way the furniture was arranged, I had to sit there looking at Chad's dick when I was trying to eat. It was like an ugly sea creature. It ruined my appetite. I'd always have to remind him to cover up with his plate or his sanitation towel. But by then, the damage to my appetite was already done.

So, I guess Unclad Chad himself could qualify as the humorous or whimsical element in the room. He also had a big giraffe that was carved out of olivewood. It was as tall as a grown man and wore a button-down shirt with a tie hanging down around its neck. It was like the wooden giraffe was more normal than Chad was.

I also saw a kitchen wall clock at some girl's parents' house once, that looked like a giant pocket watch. It was kind of goofy, if you asked me. Like having the wrong kind of timepiece up there, super-sized, was supposed to be clever. It was like having to listen to a not-that-funny joke a few times a day. Come to think of it, I didn't like this whole whimsical element idea too much. It could be that it was only meant for expensive rooms. In the poor-to-regular homes I'd seen it in so far, I thought it just looked kind of stupid.

We turned off a dirt road, into a gated entrance that had a lot of signs and warnings. Beyond the gates, there were big adobe condo buildings, with some wooden ladders on the higher-up floors, instead of steps.

"Wow. Oh, god. Yeah," Ree said, like she was enjoying the results of a man-call dance. She was grossing me out and I wanted to get out of the van. Fortunately, or possibly unfortunately, the Toe person came out to meet us then and directed us to his home. A couple of straggly dogs followed after him.

#

Ree acted like we were living in some grand palace, just because Toe's two-room condo was a thousand years old for real. It didn't even have electricity or running water. Electric and plumbing weren't allowed. I guess they'd ruin the prehistoric vibe of the place. Ree would carry drinking water in a bucket from the creek, with a faraway look on her face like she was in heaven or something. I didn't like it here because this place was supersonic boring. It was bad enough to not have TV and stuff when we were on time free but I didn't expect to still not have all that whenever we were settled. But I had to admit that when Ree was out in nature, with that look on her face, she could be in a painting at the Albuquerque Museum. Then, she somehow looked stupid, insane and beautiful, all at the same time.

I was still trying to figure out what décor would look best in Toe's prehistoric condo. Artifacts would be nice, like maybe a group of spearheads hanging on the wall, in one of those frames that had glass over it. It could also use some natural fiber things like baskets and Native blankets, maybe.

But Toe said he only wanted to stay at his prehistoric condo when a ceremony was going on there, because then his friends and relatives would come. Or else he stayed there when he didn't have anywhere else to go, like when he was married and his wife would get mad at him. He said she'd run him out of their real house with her broom and then he'd have to come stay here until she'd let him back into their real house. That was before she ran off with a butcher.

Toe would go on about that when he drank. It just slayed me to think of some woman spanking pudgy Toe with her broom, out the door and maybe even down the street. Maybe all the neighbors came out to watch. I sure would. Drunk Toe would start yelling about how his ex-wife Bernadette ran off with the butcher and I'd say, "But what about the baker? And, hey, what about the candlestick maker?" like in the old nursery rhyme.

And he'd say, "Yeah, them too, probably." Then he'd demand to fist bump. I didn't blame his wife for leaving, if she could get a better deal, which didn't seem like it would be that hard to do. Toe was mostly pretty nice but he was still a giant dum-dum.

It was his day off from his motel job so he was busy sling-shotting a bottle cap with a rubber band, then making whooshing noises as the bottle cap flew across the room. After that, he'd locate the bottle cap and do it all over again. I said, "See?" I was letting Ree know that I was right about Toe all along.

Ree just shrugged, like it didn't matter at all to her if Toe was supersonically dumb. Like she wouldn't care if she was with some guy who was dumb as an ox or a pair of socks or a box of rocks. Then again, she didn't care if she was with some guy who showed his wiener all the time like Unclad Chad, so what could I expect. Right now Ree was fashioning ugly straw dolls to sell to the clueless tourists. Tourists paid $25 apiece at the gate, just to gawk at the thousand-year-old condo complex and ask stupid questions.

They'd ask their Native guide, "Now, what kind of dances do *you* know?" like the ceremonial dances were the same as the Macarena or the Funky Chicken. I heard one guy say, "Wait, aren't y'all mostly Mexican by now?" Some of them would ask to go inside their guide's private prehistoric condo, probably to check if they had secret toilets hidden in there after all.

Toe wanted us to all go stay at his other place. His other place was really only a shack on a dirt road but at least it had TV and electricity and a bathroom. Here, you'd have to leave the prehistoric condo and walk over to the porta-potties or the real toilets by the entrance.

Ree refused to move to Toe's real house. We had to stay at the prehistoric condo because she said so, and that was that. Most of the other prehistoric condos were empty, so I didn't have anybody to hang out with, except for dum-dum Toe, when he wasn't working. There was an old church that people still went to and an old cemetery too, but they took that stuff seriously here. There was no goofing around in those places.

A few Native people had turned their condos into little shops or they'd set up a table in front of the building and sell food or crafty stuff to the tourists there. But they only did it when they felt like it. Then they'd go back to their real houses somewhere else, where they could take a shower and watch TV.

It could get a little interesting when there were tourists because they liked to ignore the rules. They'd take pictures with their phones, when they weren't allowed to. So then the tribal people would snatch their phones away. And then the tourists would get hopping mad and make threats.

The tourists didn't know that the tribe had a little jail right here that they could lock the tourists up in, if they felt like it. Nobody would let me see the jail, though. If I saw a prisoner in there, I'd have said, "You're not so smart now, are you?" Or I'd say, "Now, what have you learned from this?"

When I wasn't studying or watching for tourists to get into trouble, I messed around with the stray dogs outside and hoped I wouldn't get rabies. I tried to teach them to walk in a straight line behind me so I could be impressive but they didn't listen too well. If they didn't get a dog treat, like, every ten seconds, they'd just go lay down.

#

One Sunday after the weather warmed up, we went with Toe to a pool party at the house of some rich people he knew. We were in these people's swimming pool with a bunch of other people and Ree kept drinking the pool water and talking about how "artesian" it was, whatever that was supposed to mean. It would have been funny if it was somebody else's loony mother but it was embarrassing, since it was my loony mother and people were backing away from her.

"Mmm" Ree would say, sticking her face in the water for another big old showy slurp. Everybody got even quieter than they already were to start with. Toe's sister was there. I was hoping her name would be Finger to go with Toe, or maybe Lip or Nose, at least. But nope, it was only Winona. She offered Ree a glass of ice water from the kitchen. It was like Winona was trying to be nice, trying to quietly get Ree to stop making a fool of herself. But Ree wouldn't accept that water, she only wanted to drink the delicious, artesian swimming pool water.

Then we sat down to dinner at the tables and chairs that were set up on the patio. That is, everybody sat down except for Ree, who barged into the house instead, even though there was a little bathroom by the pool and all the food and drinks were outside too, so it didn't seem like the guests had permission to go in the house. She came back with a whole head of lettuce, then sat there eating it like an apple and saying, "Oh, yum." She loudly chomped down the whole thing, looking around now and then like she was expecting a compliment.

After that, she went around telling everybody how she made her kitchen wine and how it was also known as pruno, when nobody asked her. They'd kind of nod politely and then she'd tell them she learned to make it when she was in jail, just in case anybody didn't get it. Two of the ladies especially were looking at each other like they were having a fine time disapproving of Ree together. They raised their eyebrows and shook their heads, and then they'd kind of snicker.

I hated it when people did that. It wasn't nice. If you weren't going to try to help out with a situation, like Toe's sister had, then you should just shut up and mind your own damn business, was how I saw it. If Ree had noticed that they were making fun of her, she'd have said they were jealous because she was better looking than them. Ree was better looking than them, so you never knew, maybe that was the truth of it.

Soon after that, Toe suddenly decided it was time for us to leave the party. He and Ree had been drinking and they got into one of their dumb fights on the way back to Toe's thousand-year- old condo. I followed along with their argument, in Toe's car and after we got back home, since there was nowhere I could go to get away from it anyway. It was getting dark out. I didn't even like going outside at night to go to the porta-potty. It got pitch black out there and I'd feel the presence of sad Native ghosts all around me.

Come to find out, Toe had been bragging all over the place about his amazing new girlfriend. In his mind, the pool party was going to be his big chance to show Ree off. He'd meant to prove to everybody that, in the end, he came out way ahead of the ex-wife who'd broom spanked him and ran off with somebody else. Now he had somebody better than his ex anyway, see.

But instead of being the show-off trophy Toe had planned on, Ree got drunk and acted like a total nutbar. Toe said now they'd all be laughing at him behind his back even more than they had in the first place.

I could have told him that Ree was just a very embarrassing person. It didn't even matter that much if she was drinking or not. She didn't know how to act around domestic livestock and it was even worse when she actually wanted to fit in.

But I never would have guessed that Toe thought he had any big social position to lose. Besides not seeming very smart, he was poor, and also doughy and floppy. He also had an underbite, like the piranhas at the Albuquerque aquarium. Ree didn't go for looks though, any more than she went for money. And was a good looking person, herself. Anybody could see that. So, she was like a dating underachiever, I guess you could say. I guess it gave her the upper hand because the men she picked usually seemed ecstatic to get her, at first.

I felt kind of sorry for Toe. After all, everybody couldn't be above average. And maybe people like him were actually more worried about what other people thought than better people were anyway. Like, maybe Toe felt too close to the edge of popularity to be able to spare a single reputation molecule. It was hard to say. I felt sorry for him, either way. It was always sad when they started catching on that they didn't have what they thought they had with Ree. It was like when some poor creature thought they'd won the lottery big time, then realized they'd read the numbers wrong.

Before Toe, I don't remember Ree yelling, except sometimes at me. If whatever guy she was with said something she didn't like, she wouldn't answer him at all. Ree's silent treatments drove men nuts. She probably just didn't bother arguing with them because she knew she'd be sneaking out of their life soon, anyway. Ree and Toe liked to drink a lot together though, and then they'd fight.

Another thing that was different this time, is I didn't remember a man ever kicking us out before. Ree was the leaver and they'd be the one who was left behind. But after the pool party, Ree and Toe were yelling at each other and then Toe slapped Ree's face. He did; he hit her. It was only a soft, floppy smack but it still set my mind to buzzing.

Then I was standing there like a statue, holding my pocketknife open behind my back, waiting to see what would happen next.

I didn't have to wait long. Ree picked up Toe's prized possession, a big, heavy clay pot. She heaved it up right into Toe's face, then slammed it down hard on the floor in front of him. The pot broke into pieces. Its breaking seemed to break up the fight, too.

It was a very special pot, to Toe. We knew this. His grandmother had made it with her own hands, out of clay from the creek. I guess she must have baked it in one of the big bread ovens outside. It was special because she'd made it herself and now she was dead.

Toe left the big pottery pieces on the floor. He slunk down into his usual chair at the table, like the booze and anger had been drained from him. I thought he might say he was sorry then or maybe not say anything and just go to bed. But what he said was, "Get out."

Ree looked startled for a second. Then she starting packing, real quick. She motioned for me to do the same. Toe never looked up from the table.

#

So there we were, back on the road, that fast. Ree seemed excited, dancing around in her seat while she drove, singing along with that Redbone song, "Come and Get Your Love." It reminded me of Rex and Harley, and Ree yanking me out of my life in Albuquerque. The music might have lightened Ree's mood but it didn't lighten mine.

She drove to another one of her abandoned shacks. She went straight there, like she already had it picked out.

I had a bad feeling about the place as soon as I saw it in the van's headlights. It was more than my usual dislike of the time free places. This was a supersonic bad vibe. But that wouldn't make any difference to Ree. So I just sat there feeling like something really, really bad was going to happen and there was nothing I could do but wait for it.

We slept in the van that night and the next. I wanted to keep sleeping in the van, if we had to stay out here alone in the middle of nowhere. I always wanted to sleep in the van on time free because at least a bad guy couldn't sneak up on you without warning like they could if you were in a structure without any door locks, if there was even a door. In the van, we could also more easily just leave, if there was any trouble. We could just drive away.

Ree said no, no, no, about continuing to sleep in the van, like she always did. According to her, it would be bad to get used to relying on the van for shelter, for some reason. We'd gotten the shack cleaned out now and that's where we had to sleep.

So we dragged our sleeping bags in there and unrolled them. I turned and faced the wall since I felt like I hated Ree right then, even though it hadn't been her choice to leave this time. My bad feeling about the place turned out to be so, so right.

After Ree fell asleep, I was still awake, tensing up at every sound, even before the low, steady droning started up. It was more than just sound, though. The ground vibrated a little under me too, like a train was passing by. But there was no train and it didn't pass by. It just went on and on, the low, steady droning and the low, steady shaking.

Ree slept through it all but after a few hours of the creepy noise that I felt as well as heard, I thought I was going to lose my mind. It was dark and eerie, like something from the underworld.

Finally, I was exhausted enough that I dropped off to sleep for a few minutes at a time anyway. And that's when the dead woman appeared, the one Juno and I saw in that old shed in Albuquerque.

A vision of her materialized in front of me, a ghost or apparition or whatever you'd call such a horror. She had the same long black hair, the leathery skin, the blue flannel shirt. She was in an upright position but floating in the air, a couple of feet higher up off the ground than she'd have been if she was standing there, alive.

I screamed until Ree woke up. She rushed me out to the van, and then I couldn't stop shivering.

I made Ree drive away from there and keep driving, until we finally came to a truck stop along the highway, where there were bright lights and other people around. We went into the truck stop's 24 hour café. Ree ordered me a country fried steak with mashed potatoes and a chocolate shake, without me even asking for it. And she didn't once say anything about it being domestic livestock feed.

Away from that horrid shack, back to civilization and with a full stomach, I calmed down some.

Ree said, "Now, what was all that about? Tell me." Her face was worried, soft, which was strange for Ree. I must have seemed dangerously insane.

I said, "I heard humming. And vibrating. Like, for hours."

"Ah, okay. I bet that was the Taos hum. It's a thing around here. Nobody seems to know what causes it, and, apparently, only some people can hear it. That's what I've heard."

That made me feel a touch better, like I hadn't completely lost my mind. But then, that was nowhere near the worst part of it. I said, "I never heard of a Taos hum. But also... I saw a ghost. A dead lady, who I've seen in real life."

I'd sort of made myself forget about the dead lady but I guessed she still weighed heavy on me, deep in my mind. I couldn't carry that secret anymore. It was driving me over the edge.

Ree said, "You saw a lady in real life. But in your... vision, she was dead?"

"No. She was dead when I saw her in real life." I broke into tears again but this time, without screaming.

"You saw a dead woman?"

I nodded, face in my hands.

"Where? Did you guys go to a funeral in Albuquerque, when I was... away working?"

"No. My friend and I went into an old abandoned shed and the dead lady was in there."

Ree rummaged around in her pouch for her tobacco stuff. She fixed herself a pipe and lit it, which was not allowed. After a slow puff, she said, "What did you girls do then? Did you report it?"

I shook my head. No, we did not report it.

"Hmm. And do you want to report it?"

"Oh, I have to report it. It's the only way I can think of that might keep the ghost from coming to me again. I mean, aren't ghosts something to do with unfinished business? Right?"

Ree said, "Let me think for a minute." She asked the waitress for more ice water and the check. The waitress stood there looking at the smoke coming from Ree's pipe,

like she was about to say something. But then she went
away.

Ree said, "Do you know what street this shed was on?
Or anything else that could help someone find it, like
businesses near it, any landmarks, anything like that?"

"I could probably find it on the phone."

She passed me her phone. When the waitress came back,
Ree handed her some cash.

"It's sort of in here," I showed her the map on the screen.
"See, there's the taco stand. The house the shed belongs to
is abandoned. It's like a green color and has empty land on
both sides of it."

"All right. Give me that. I'll go to that pay phone over
there and call it in. You wait here."

She emptied her pipe into her water glass.

I watched her at the pay phone, twirling the cord in her
fingers. After a while, she came back. She said, "All done.
Better?"

"Much better. Thanks," I said, though those few words
hardly seemed like enough, for her getting that terrible
secret off my conscience at last.

Outside, the darkness of night was lifting. It was nearly
dawn. Ree hurried me to the van.

She said, "Let's get out of here. I bet a lot of drug deals
go down on those truck stop pay phones. The cops might
have them tapped."

We sped down the highway for a while. Then she said,
"How would you feel about staying at another campground
for a while? I heard of one that even has pay showers and a
laundromat. And there are plenty of other people around.
Better?"

I nodded. "Thanks, Bonnie Sue," I said. *Oh shit.* "Sorry.
Um, it's just been a mixed up night."

After a tense minute, Ree seemed to accept that, no doubt only letting me off the hook because of the traumatic night I'd just been through. The truth was though, Ree had just acted like an excellent mother, for a change. Like Bonnie Sue.

#

Ree had helped Toe with his side hustle of making things to sell to tourists, and now she kept making stuff without him, at the campground. I tried not to think about how Ree's man-call activities got us kicked out of the last campground we'd stayed at. That was right before we went to stay with Toe, or Totem Pole, as Ree called him now, the couple of times she mentioned him at all.

I didn't think of it at the time but Ree must have paid to stay in that last campground, too. She had definitely changed some. But then I guessed I had changed some, too. Her changes weren't enough, though. We were still itinerant. *I-tin-erant. Rant. Errant?* I grabbed Ree's phone from the old blanket we were sitting on. Ree had stuck a board she'd found somewhere over the fire grate, turning it into a tabletop that we used as a work surface. I typed in the word. *Errant- Erring or straying from the proper course or standards.* That was us, all right. No, that was Ree. I was just a hostage or something.

Itinerant-

Someone whose way of life involves traveling around. Usually someone who is poor and

homeless.

Synonyms:

transient, nomad, gypsy, drifter, vagrant, tramp, bird of passage.

Bird of passage. I kind of liked that one. It sounded pretty.

Taos got a lot of rich tourists, even though a lot of them looked like old hippies, until you checked out the brand names on their hippie clothes and stuff. Ree kept trying out new products on them and making adjustments, depending on what sold well and what she made the most profit on. She played music on her phone a lot and sang along, classic rock, country, and her chanting and drumming stuff, like those creepy Gregorian chants that sounded like the perfect background music for the Taos hum. Ree put music on when she was happy.

To sell her stuff, she'd spread out a blanket on the square and arrange her merchandise on it. It seemed like every New Mexico town was laid out the same way, which I thought was just how all towns were laid out until Ree said no, that was just New Mexico. There was always a town square, the oldest part of town, with lots of adobe buildings. That was originally where everybody in town lived, a century or two ago. Nowadays, that would be the tourist part of town, with restaurants and pricey little shops that sold silver and Native art and homemade soap.

Outside on the sidewalks there would be local people selling stuff on their own. Some of Ree's best sellers were her southwest spice mixes and southwest cocoa mixes. She'd buy huge containers of herbs, spices and cocoa powder, mix them up, then put the dry mixes into jars that she bought by the dozen. Finally, she'd slap old fashioned looking labels on them.

She also sold her own cookbook of Taos recipes now, with ingredients like blue corn, pinon nuts, Hatch chili peppers and calabacita. She found the recipes online, then switched the ingredients around some, so no one could say she was copying.

When the tarantulas were out on the prowl during their mating season, Ree collected them. She sold them in tiny plastic cages that had each tarantula's name on it, along with a list of instructions on tarantula care. There was Taos the tarantula, of course. And Terrence, Tarzan, Tarik and Tehran. The spiders she found, mostly by the sides of the roads, were males. It was the males who were on the move, looking for females to mate with. But before she knew that, she gave half of them girl names: Tara, Tulip, Tori. The spiders with girl names sold better, so she kept on with it anyway.

Her latest thing was small, quickie watercolor paintings of mountains and pine trees and stuff. The designs were also from the internet. She painted them herself, then put them into frames from Walmart. She signed them "Ann O'Keeffe," a sly hint that they just might have been painted by a relative of Georgia O'Keeffe's.

Her latest thing was dying her hair black. Trying to look Native, I guess. The rich tourists wanted authentic stuff from the locals. I said, "So, you're Georgie O'Keeffe's Native relative, really?"

"That's show biz, kid."

"It's not, though. It's really not show biz."

"Hush up and stick these labels on those chili cocoa jars. Put them on straight."

"All right. Fine."

Ree seemed jazzed about hawking her overpriced gifty souvenirs. It didn't seem very Ree-like to me. But when I asked her about it, she said, "The only constant in life is change."

"Yeah, especially when you constantly change life yourself, for no good reason." It came out harsher than I meant and I cringed as soon as I said it. We'd been having a good day together, which was kind of rare lately.

"Listen kid, I'm trying, okay? I'm trying, for you. You've got that label on crooked, dammit. Do it over."

"Sorry," I said, apologizing for more than the crooked label. Sort of.

#

When Ree went outside the van I grabbed a ten dollar bill from the glove box, for the Sunflower café. I snitched money from the glove box all the time now. I figured part of it was mine, since I helped a lot with the tourist stuff Ree made. And she had extra money now. Her merchandise was selling well and she hardly spent anything for us to live. I could probably have supported us like this on the money I used to get just for helping Lella with her kids. Ree wouldn't give me any, though. Not a dime. So I just took it.

At the Sunflower café, they had a lounge section where you could hang out. There were couches, tables, board games and a TV. I loved getting away from the campsite and being around other people, like somebody with a real life.

I bought a Zia brand Nopales-something soda. They didn't sell Coke here, only local stuff. It was good soda, once you got it through your head that it was supposed to be different from the kind of soda you were used to.

There was nobody in the lounge section, so I settled in on a couch to watch TV. Man, I loved TV. The boring news was on though and I didn't know if changing the channel was allowed.

I was sipping my cactus soda and trying to decide if I should just go ahead and change the channel, or go find somebody to ask first, or just settle for watching the boring news. That's what I was thinking about when Cyrus's face popped up on the TV screen.

It was Juno's older brother Cyrus, who I'd had my first kiss from back in Albuquerque. Well, it was only a practice kiss and Juno made him do it, but still. There was his police mug shot, filling the TV screen, while the news lady talked about a missing woman and an anonymous tip.

Then the old shed that the body was in popped up on the screen, with the old house in the background. In honor of the dead woman, the city planned to knock down the house and the shed. It took me a while to figure out because they called knocking the house and shed down "razing" them, which sounded like "raising," which didn't make any sense.

So that was the real reason the dead woman was a big secret? *Cyrus killed her?* Did Juno know? Of course Juno didn't know. I really doubted that. Juno was the best friend I ever had. But why did she even know about it, in the first place? I wondered if Cyrus told her about it or if she overheard something or what. Not that it really mattered now.

I thought about the terrifying visit I'd had from the dead lady. After the whole topic had time to sink into my mind, I wanted more than anything to just get away from that TV. I didn't want to hear any more, not one more word. I got up and ran all the way back to our van, without stopping.

Ree was nowhere around at the campsite so I got in the van and checked that all the doors were locked, then got into my sleeping bag. I hid in it, on the back floor of the van and shivered, though it was a warm day.

I had a deep feeling then, more a knowing really, that the ghost visit I'd had the night of the Taos hum was meant to bring about exactly what happened. Like the dead woman showed herself to jog my conscience. Like it was her way of getting me to tell.

At the same time I'd felt such heavy guilt for not telling about the dead woman, it also seemed to me that it might have been kinder to never tell, to let the loved ones keep some hope. Let them think she might come back some day, that she probably just ran off with the circus or something and was out there having a ball somewhere. Who would want to get the horrifying news that poor lady's family received? The times I didn't know where Ree was, I didn't like it at all but I'm pretty sure it would have been way worse to find out she was dead. That was my opinion about it.

Either way, hidden, murdered corpses and real life visits from their spirits weren't easy things to know about firsthand. They just weren't.

#

I went back to the Sunflower café a couple of days later. After all, what I saw on the news at the cafe didn't have anything to do with anybody there. I bought another Zia soda, watermelon-something this time, and took it to the lounge area.

I pretended in my mind that I'd come to a bar to meet a handsome guy and that my soda was a beer. The beer part was easy to do, since the soda came in a dark brown bottle. I liked thinking about meeting a guy a lot better than thinking about the last time I was here. I hoped nobody would ask why I'd run away after barely even touching my drink.

A tall, sandy-haired guy with a sly crooked smile was the only other one in the lounge area. He was watching a re-run of *I Love Lucy* on the TV. With his gaze on me, I felt crazy, like I wanted to kiss his smart-alecky looking mouth, then run away or something. It shocked me, though. Here I was pretending I was there to meet a handsome guy and now a handsome guy was right here looking at me, like I'd just ordered him off the menu. Then again, I thought about meeting a handsome guy all the time lately. Every day, probably.

I just said hi, then sat down on the couch opposite to the one he was on. He said hi back and then we made some awkward small talk on the commercials, about what our names were (his was Devon) and where we lived (he lived with his mom) and stuff like that. Talking to good looking guys or, really, anybody in my age group seemed strange to me. I wasn't used to it anymore.

We played a few games of checkers and I reminded myself not to rub it in whenever I'd win a round. After that, we took a walk, just around the parking lot and stuff. Then he said he had to go help with some home repair job because his boss would be expecting him.

Some old man was walking by and Devon asked him to take our picture. Outside the Sunflower café, there was a large board with big sunflowers painted on it. There were holes cut out in the middles of the sunflowers, where you could stick your face through from behind, for photos. The photo itself was goofy, but I was jazzed that Devon wanted a photo of the two of us. Devon's face was in the middle of an orange sunflower and my face, a little lower down, was in the middle of a yellow sunflower.

I headed back to the campsite, wound up, feeling all floaty and swoony, practically like I was in love already. I hadn't felt like this about anybody since Reeve Salazar came back in Albuquerque. But that was just kid stuff. Devon was a grown man with a job. Well, he was sixteen, two years older than me, which was kind of a lot. But he was still school age at least, not some adult weirdo. It was almost like he was completely grown though because he'd quit school to work a full-time job.

I was supposed to meet him back at the Sunflower at two o'clock on Saturday. I didn't know if we were going somewhere from there, like on a real date, or if he just meant we'd hang out at the café again. I didn't care, either way. I just wanted to see him again. But I wished I knew if jeans and sneakers would be okay should or if I should get dressed up. If so, then another problem was that I didn't have any dressy clothes.

But why did he suddenly say he had to leave? Was there really somewhere he had to be or had he changed his mind about me and just said that to get rid of me? But then, if he was trying to ditch me, why would he bother with the sunflower photo? My questions circled round and round in my mind, finding no answers.

I'd have given anything to talk to Juno right then. She'd know how to read the situation and she'd know what to do about the clothes thing, too. Or she'd at least have some thoughts on it all, if nothing else. I was sorry I'd never tried to call her before, in the two-plus years since I had to leave Albuquerque. I didn't even say good-bye.

At the time, though, there hadn't seemed to be much reason to keep in touch with somebody I'd probably never see again. Besides, then I'd have had to explain why I was suddenly gone, which was embarrassing or exhausting or something. But then I remembered that there was more to it than that. I knew even then that Juno and I would probably be going our separate ways soon anyway, because of the secret. I doubted you could share something like that for long and just keep hanging out and having fun together. It was too dark and heavy to have sitting between you, the kind of thing you just wanted to get far away from.

It was too late for our friendship now, anyway. I'd told the secret, after swearing that I wouldn't. The secret that she wasn't supposed to tell me, in the first place. And now her brother was locked up, probably for the rest of his life. I was glad I told, though. If he killed that lady, then screw him. He'd deserve whatever he got. But I was also pretty sure Juno would never want to hear from me again.

#

On our first date, Devon and I didn't just hang out at the Sunflower café'. We went for a drive, stopping for a bite to eat along the way, something we've done a lot since then. After that first date, we just seemed to be a couple. We didn't have any talk about being exclusive like I'd seen on the internet, we just went on a date and then we were together.

That wasn't hard for me, since I didn't know anybody else to go out with anyway. Since Reeve Salazar in the sixth grade, the closest I'd come to connecting with any guy besides Devon was when a strange male would look me up and down in the square but that kind of thing seemed more like a threat than an invitation to me. And even that had only happened a couple of times, anyway. I didn't draw a lot of male attention like Ree did. I was just regular looking.

Ree was outside the van now, looking like a vampiress at the moment, with her black hair and pale skin. She was stringing small, colorful beads into long necklaces to sell. It bugged me how her poncho kept slipping down off her shoulder and how she kept stopping what she was doing to yank it back up.

When she finished with a necklace, she'd wind it around one of the stiff cards that she'd had printed up with the words *Love Beads* on them. She thought the plastic beads might not be upscale enough for the rich hippies but decided to try a small batch of them anyway.

Since she was outside, I waited for Devon inside the van. Ree and I did that a lot, one of us staying in the van and the other one outside. It was like having a two-room house that way, I guess. Otherwise, we'd practically be sitting in each other's laps all the time.

Devon pulled up in his truck. He and Ree didn't like each other. Ree hadn't seemed that interested in me until Devon came along, and then she suddenly wanted me all to herself. And Devon thought Ree was a bad influence on me. I'd griped to him about her too much, before I realized he'd want to involve himself in it.

But Devon didn't call Ree names or make rude comments like she did to him. He just didn't talk to her at all, if he didn't have to. He got out of his truck to come knock on the van door but Ree said, "Oh, hello there, devil Devon. Developmentally delayed Devon. Deviled egg head."

I couldn't help but laugh. It was so immature and stupid that it cracked me up.

Devon turned around and got back in his truck. He honked his horn to let me know he was waiting for me.

Ree always had to say something to him.

"Be nice," I said to her, on my way to Devon's truck.

"You too, soccer mom Suzy."

We headed out of the campground and Devon said, "Did she call you a soccer mom? What the hell is that supposed to mean?"

"I don't know. Just that she thinks I'm boring, I guess."

"Why, because you don't pull trains like she does?"

"What does that mean?" I grabbed one of his Marlboros out of the pack and lit it.

"Star. That "man-call" bullshit. She's hooking. You know that, right?"

"Hooking what? What's that?"

He shook his head. "Damn. I've got to get you out of there."

"What? I know she has sex with a group of men at a time sometimes. I think it's gross but I just go wait in the van or whatever." His anger bored me. I didn't want to talk about my mother. I wanted to talk about our love. Or at least about where he was driving me to right now.

"There's something wrong with her."

It seemed he'd be stuck on this topic for a while again, so I grabbed his phone and typed *pulling a train*. After exhaling a mouthful of smoke, I read: *Having sex with a line of people*. "Why would they have to be in a line? Hey, why don't you get one of those vape things? Then we could smoke different flavors."

He said, "Okay. Maybe. I don't know. See how much they cost."

I typed in *hooking*. "It says *Restraining an opponent with one's hockey stick*. Oh, wait. Here it is: *Having sex for money*. I don't think she gets paid. That would be smarter, though."

"Smarter? You think prostitution is smart, then? You admire it?" Now he was getting mad.

"I don't know. I think you admire it. You're the one who can't stop thinking about it." He was the one who started this stupid conversation in the first place.

"Yeah, it's all a big joke, until." He was wound up and kept ranting.

I decided to ignore him, like Ree did when whoever she was with got on her nerves. I grabbed another cigarette from his pack and lit it, and watched the bighorn sheep as we rode by. If I didn't know better, I'd have thought they were big goats, not sheep.

I put on some music, then set his phone back down and sang along, sort of guessing at the lyrics. It was a beautiful day, with the leaves turning orange and red and the air scented like pine and... cinnamon?

He said, "Did you hear me?"

A while later, he said, "Why aren't you answering me?"

Then, "Are you mad? Hey, I'm just looking out for you. Because I love you."

"You love me?" Finally, he said something interesting.

"Why. Don't you love me?"

"Yes. I guess. When you're nice."

"I'm always nice to you, babe. You just don't always understand that. Hey, I know, I'm gonna get you a phone. Yeah. I don't know why I didn't think of it before. Then if Ree – or anybody else- starts getting weird, you call me."

Ah, the magic of the silent treatment. See, I'd been just about to say, "Back off, jack off," one of my best lines when he stuck his nose too far into my business. But I stayed silent instead. And then he'd told me he loved me and promised me a phone. Ka-boom!

On the inside, I was jumping up and down with joy. *A phone, a phone, a phone!* But he didn't need to know that. He needed to remember to think twice, the next time he wanted to talk at me instead of to me. I said, "Okay. But what about the vape?"

He made a funny face then and blew a raspberry, so I decided to settle for his love and a phone, for now.

The gorge bridge was awesome, so long and so high above the Rio Grande. I'd never been on it before, unless it was when I was asleep in Ree's van or something and just didn't remember it. But once we were out in the middle of the bridge, looking down was scary, especially since it didn't seem like there was even that much water in the river below. If you went over the edge, the water wouldn't help you. This was probably what it was like to fly in an airplane.

Up ahead, a car was stopped on the bridge, partly on the narrow shoulder and partly blocking our lane. A girl got out of the driver's side of the parked car. She walked around her car to the narrow walkway on the side of the bridge and gripped the railing with both hands. She leaned over it.

"Son of a bitch. She's gonna jump," Devon said, as my stomach lurched. He pulled over and put the truck in park. He opened his door.

"Let me do it," I said, before I realized it. For some reason, I felt like a strange guy approaching her might scare her right over the edge or something. This was a job for me.

He said, "All right, then. But don't get too close. She might try to take you with her."

I didn't know what to say to her and there was no time to think it over. I kept my voice deliberately slow and friendly though, not wanting to alarm her. "Hey, there. Can you come and talk to me for a while? I really wish you would."

She turned toward me. Her eyes looked wild, scared.

I held my hands out in her direction, palms up, moving a couple of baby steps closer to her. "Let's go get something to eat and just talk for a while. Let's be friends."

She didn't answer me. But she seemed to be thinking about it.

Then she turned back to the bridge rail and put her foot up on it. I forced myself to keep my voice slow and steady, though my stomach churned and my head was full of bees. "My name is Star. What's yours? Please come and talk to me. Just for a minute, at least."

She turned back to me, then looked out over the Rio Grande again. It seemed like she sort of wanted to change her course of action, but wasn't quite sure yet.

"Let's go get a bite to eat. I'll pay. Would you?" It seemed like staying very calm was very necessary. I hoped she couldn't tell that my teeth were chattering.

Finally, she did. She turned away from the bridge railing and walked over to me. She said, simply, "My name is Olivia."

Devon swooped in and grabbed her, and she started yelling. I wasn't sure it was necessary. But above her yelling, I yelled, "It's okay, Olivia. He's just making sure you're safe. Don't worry."

Devon wrestled her to his truck and we got her seated in there, in the middle, in case she changed her mind and decided to try to jump out when the truck was moving.

She seemed to give up on fighting against us. She just sat there while I buckled her in, like you'd do with a small child.

Devon said, "All right. We're all just gonna sit here a minute and calm down, okay? And then we'll go get something to eat. Now, who wants a smoke?"

Oh god. Was he really offering this chick a lit cigarette right now? What if she, like, decided to stick it in her eye? Or burn one of us. I mean, though we had good cause, we'd still just sort of kidnapped her. I really, really wanted a cigarette myself right then, though. I said, "I do."

"Me, too," Olivia said.

The three of us smoked, with the windows only partway down, since Devon and I didn't trust the girl not to make a wild escape attempt.

Then Devon drove us to McDonald's. I kept my gaze strictly away from the hideously long drop on both sides of the bridge.

At McDonald's, we sat there eating and talking. Olivia didn't seem like she might make a break for it, though I still didn't trust her completely on that. It seemed that she liked us, though. I'd heard one time that if you ever felt suicidal, you should focus on three basics right away: food, sleep and a shower, things that usually make anybody feel better.

I didn't remember where I'd heard that but I figured it couldn't hurt. So I kept offering Olivia more food. And I kept eating too, so she wouldn't think I was treating her like a mental patient or anything.

She didn't seem to want to talk about what had just gone down or what led to it, so we were all kind of doing this act like everything was just fine.

After my third trip back to the counter in an hour, Olivia and I each having ordered a Big Mac, a fish sandwich, a cheeseburger, large fries and a shake. Devon gave me a look. He was careful with his money, now that he was saving to get his own place. Olivia went to the restroom and I had a minute to explain my reasoning to him.

He said, "Ah, gotcha. But what are we gonna do with her now, babe?"

"Hold that thought, babe. I better go check on her."

When Olivia and I returned to the table, we continued talking about regular stuff, like where we were from (Me: Roswell, originally. Devon: Born and raised right here in Taos. Olivia: Santa Fe).

We talked about our middle names. Mine's Dee, a compromise, since Ree had wanted to name me Desert Star, before my dad supposedly said it was a stripper name. Then, according to what I heard Bonnie Sue tell Brynn's mom back in Roswell, Ree tried for "Star Desert" but my dad said that was just a backwards stripper name. This got a smile from Olivia and a glare from Devon.

I said, "Babe, don't start that shit." Then Olivia raised her eyebrows and Devon and I both shut up. The last thing we needed was to argue in front of Olivia and get her upset right now. I finished my story, though now I wished I hadn't brought it up. I explained that my middle name ended up being Dee because it was the first letter of "Desert."

The story didn't sound right to me, though, or at least the part where my dad supposedly took a big stand against a name and put his foot down. I didn't remember him taking a big stand about anything. But maybe Big Mom-Mom made him do it or Bonnie Sue just heard it wrong.

Devon's middle name was Isaac, which was kind of funny because his last name was Miller, so his initials spelled "dim." He said, "Whatever you do, please don't tell Ree that."

I said to Olivia, "Ree is my mother. She teases Devon about his name."

She said, "Yeah, don't tell her that, then haha. My middle name's boring. It's just May."

Devon said, "Oh yeah? Olivia may what?"

I felt bad then because it seemed like a kind of sex-related comment. Devon didn't need to worry about what Olivia may do. He should only joke like that with me, not other girls.

After a while, Devon said, "Son of a bitch. We forgot about Olivia's car. It might get towed."

"Oh, gosh. You're right," Olivia said. "Can we go get it now?"

Devon and I exchanged a look. Olivia didn't need to be anywhere near that bridge again today. He said, "Hmm. I know, let me call my buddy, Raul. If he's around, he and I can get the car and bring it to Star's place. How about if I drop you two off there, either way. If Raul's not around, I'll grab somebody else. Then… we'll all go bowling?"

Olivia said that all sounded great to her. She seemed real normal for someone who had tried to off herself an hour and a half ago. I said, "I've never been bowling before." I was surprised Devon was up for spending more money tonight.

"Ooh, more virgin territory, then?" Devon said to me. I laughed along with it a little but now I was really mad. He didn't need to make little sexy jokes to another girl or hint at my personal business in front of her, either. Especially when Olivia was seventeen, even older than Devon. She'd probably done the deed lots of times.

To change the subject, I told Olivia not to forget to give Devon her car keys.

She did, and then she said, "Oh, gosh. I left my purse in the car, too. I've had such a good time talking to you guys that I forgot all about it. It's been a while since I hung out with people and stuff."

I wasn't sure which way to go with her. It would be wonderful to have a best friend again, like Juno. And it would be super cool to have a best friend who was practically grown. But at the same time, I didn't want Olivia to think she was Devon's best friend, too. She was a pretty girl. I could tell Devon noticed it, too. I hated being jealous. It was such a horrible feeling. I decided to give Olivia a small chance but not get too attached to her. I'd just see how it went.

Devon dropped me and Olivia off at the campsite. On the way there, we'd decided that Olivia should spend the night with me in the van, if Ree allowed it, since we didn't have any better ideas. I hoped Ree would be nice.

Ree was outside, in one of the lawn chairs she'd bought. Buying lawn chairs was the kind of thing she'd have laughed at before, if somebody else did it. Some man was sitting in the other lawn chair. I didn't see him at first. They had the fire going, with two steaks and two potatoes on the grill. This could be a good sign. It was getting too cold out for van life, if you asked me. Ree never seemed to notice the weather, though.

I said, "This is Olivia. Um, can she stay here with us, at least for tonight? She needs somewhere to stay." I figured Ree was more likely to say yes if I put her on the spot in front of her new man.

"Sure. No problem. Welcome to my humble abode, Olivia." Ree was in a good mood. She sounded a little drunk. She and the man were drinking beer. The man was sneakily looking Olivia up and down now. He better watch it. Unclad Chad had hell to pay for that kind of thing, when he didn't even do it.

Olivia said, "Nice to meet you, Ree. And thank you."

Ree didn't introduce the man. Not that there was much reason to. He was obviously some guy she'd just met, who would soon either go away or let us move into his house.

Olivia and I stood around for a few minutes. I could have gotten the old blanket and Olivia and I could sit on it, on the ground by the fire, but I didn't really feel invited. Or we could sit in the van but I was tired of sitting in the van.

I said to Olivia, "Want to wait for the guys at the Sunflower café? They have TV."

To Ree, I said, "Devon and his friend will be bringing Olivia's car by. Can you tell them we're at the café?"

"You got it," she said, but she seemed too giggly about it to be trusted. So I picked up her phone and called Devon myself.

Later on, bowling was fun, after I accepted that I was the worst one by far, and that was just how it was going to go. I quit worrying about all my gutter balls. Since meeting Devon, my world grew larger all the time. And now he was talking about getting his own place and me moving in with him. The idea thrilled and terrified me.

I'd only met Devon's friend Raul once before, real quick when we ran into him at Kentucky Fried Chicken. Devon knew him from his construction job. Raul was older, like nineteen, and he already had his own apartment. He and Olivia seemed to be hitting it off really well. They even kissed already. I was super happy about that. Olivia would fit into my life a lot better if she had a boyfriend of her own.

She didn't spend the night with me and Ree in the van, though. She went home with Raul. They must have stopped at the campsite and picked up Olivia's car, because it was gone when Devon dropped me off.

On the way home to the campsite, Devon and I talked about if he should tell Raul about Olivia's suicide attempt. We couldn't decide, one way or the other. So we decided we'd talk about it some more the next day.

#

Devon and I were on a special date for our three month anniversary. He said he wanted to take me to a fancy restaurant and he even gave me a couple hundred dollars to buy an outfit for it.

Olivia took me shopping for a dress earlier in the week. The four of us had hung out a few more times as couples but that was the first time it was just me and Olivia. I couldn't tell if she wanted to be closer friends with me or if the guys had just asked her to take me shopping. She was nice enough but she didn't talk very much or seem to want to hang out more after the shopping was done. She said she had to go do something right then and maybe she did.

Devon and I decided to mind our own business about finding Olivia on the bridge, for two reasons. One was because Devon decided he wasn't obligated to. He hadn't known Raul all that well, before the four of us started getting together. Raul had only been a work buddy. So Devon guessed such a warning wouldn't be expected.

The other reason was that Olivia never left Raul's apartment after she went home with him, the night we all went bowling. So, while Devon and I were still thinking about it, they quickly become a couple. So telling now might seem like butting into their relationship. Or maybe we were just chicken. If it ever came up, Devon would say he'd just figured the two of them had already talked about it. It was a tricky situation.

I dressed all in red for our big date. Devon had said he liked me in red and I was lucky enough to find a red dress I liked. I wore my new red sweater dress, red tights and red high heels. Plus, I carried a red purse and wore a red fabric flower in my hair.

After I bought all that with Olivia's help, she took me to Walmart for cosmetics. She said they cost too much at the other places. She helped me pick out a whole face full: foundation, blush, lipstick, eyeshadow, eyeliner, and mascara. And a pair of glittery, fake diamond and silver earrings, when we finally found some clip-ons. The ear piercings I got with Bonnie Sue and Big Mom-Mom were closed up at the backs of my earlobes. I might be able to fix them by sticking a needle through the piercings but I was nervous enough about my upcoming fancy date just then without sticking needles into myself, too.

It was embarrassing to even say this in my own mind, for some reason, but after I got ready for my date, in makeup and a dress, I felt grown up and beautiful.

When I was ready to go, Ree said, "Little red riding hood meets the big, bad wolf." Then she stood there with a sour look on her face. I was glad when Devon pulled up and I could escape.

In the restaurant waiting area, Devon made me turn all around so he could see how I looked from every angle, while he whistled. I felt like a million bucks.

Now, at the table, he kept looking at me like he was surprised and impressed. His feelings seemed real. Makeup sure made a difference. Instead of just a regular face, my eyes and lips were emphasized. Decorating myself seemed a lot like decorating a room. You could make a regular place or a regular face into something noteworthy, with the right paint and upholstery. I'd never worn make-up before, aside from kiddie lip gloss. I hoped I did it right. I just kept it light, figuring I couldn't go too wrong that way.

Dorado's was the nicest place I'd ever eaten at, by far, and I was afraid I'd do something stupid. But after we got settled in and Devon placed our order, I got into the mood of it and I calmed down.

The restaurant had lots of stone and wrought iron and the people working there wore black suits. A fireplace took up almost a whole wall. We also had candlelight at our table and, before the sun dropped, a stunning view of the snowy mountains, while we were toasty warm in the glamorous dining room.

Devon was dressed up, too, with a button-down shirt and pants that weren't jeans. He said, "I have some news that you might like, babe."

"Oh really? What is it?"

"I got my own place. I'm moving next weekend."

"Wow! Are you serious? How? Where?"

"It's over in Arroyo Seco. It's nothing big, just a studio apartment above a little restaurant there. The lady who owns it is a friend of Raul's family. She didn't even ask for my ID or anything."

"That's amazing! Oh, wait. What did your mom say?"

"Ha. Nothing. Because she doesn't know."

"Really? But what if she calls the cops or something?"

"Nah, it's all good. There's not enough room at her house anyway, since my sister moved in with her kid."

"Oh. Well, congratulations, babe." I held my water glass up and we toasted. I'd never met Raul's mom or his sister, Roxanne. When Devon told them about me, they ganged up on him about how a fourteen-year-old, me, was too young to date.

He didn't feel like listening to any more of it, so then he just didn't bring me up to them anymore. His mom and sister had each had a kid before they were sixteen so, if you asked me, they didn't have any room to talk.

But after that, Devon and I promised each other not to tell anybody else my real age. If anybody asked, we'd say I was sixteen, the same as Devon, not fourteen. My age hadn't come up with Raul and Olivia yet. But if they asked, that's what we'd say.

After the toast, Devon said, "Thank you, gorgeous. Like I said, it's a small place, nothing fancy. But I can make room for you."

"Thanks, babe." I didn't say more than that because I didn't know what to say. However small his apartment was, I was pretty sure it was bigger than the van I lived in now, and more comfortable, too.

I floated off in my mind all the time lately, thinking about living with Devon, romantic daydreams like spooning together to go to sleep. I always pictured it under an open window for some reason, with moonlight shining in on us. But at the same time, I just couldn't picture telling Ree that I was leaving her.

And then, there was that other problem. That sex thing that I had to get out of the way. Whether I moved in with Devon right away or not, he was getting tired of waiting. Devon was practically a grown man. He wouldn't wait forever for full sex.

I chose some fancy taco platter and just ice water to drink. I got one of the cheaper meals, though nothing on this menu was actually cheap. Devon needed his money for his start in life, for our start.

On this special romantic occasion, in these elegant surroundings, I'd just about made up my mind to tell Devon I'd go all the way with him. May as well get it over with and then I wouldn't have to worry about it anymore.

I looked up at him, shy-like to make it extra sexy and opened my mouth to tell him.

But before I could say it, he started getting giddy and goofy, I guess from the joy of being here on this elegant anniversary date and because he was getting his own apartment. It seemed like he was the most obnoxious when he was the happiest. He started teasing me about the huitlacoche, an ingredient that was listed on the menu as being included in my taco filling.

"Do you know what it is?" he said, his teeth pretty in the candlelight, framed by that crooked, smart-alecky smile.

"No. I can't even pronounce it. Um, is it some kind of beef seasoning, maybe?"

"Noooo."

He looked very happy about it. I said, "Some kind of pepper or something? I don't know."

"It's corn fungus. Fungus! Like, mildew that grows on corn." He smiled hugely, like he was overjoyed to inform me that I was eating mildew.

"Eww." I looked inside my tacos but I couldn't see any fungus, or any other single ingredient, for that matter. The taco filling ingredients were all chopped up and mixed together.

"Yep. When you think about it, you're pretty much eating corn smegma, babe."

"What's that?" He sat there smiling, so I keyed it in on my phone.

Ugh. Sometimes he was so immature. He kept at it, corn smegma, corn mold, corn snot, cum and diarrhea. It grossed me out and ruined my appetite. I carefully ate around the tacos, spooning up only the rice and squash side dishes. He thought that was hilarious, too.

I suddenly sort of wanted to go home. But I tried to get past it. A lot of times with Devon, there would be a low spot somewhere in with all the fun and lovey stuff. Giving your heart to someone was hard. Little things could make you feel like somebody just knocked you over, in a way that would hardly ever happen with a girl pal.

After Devon finished his tamales, he ate my tacos, too. I wondered if that was his plan all along. I changed my mind about telling him we could go all the way. I played a game on my phone like he wasn't even there. But he was too busy talking about which dessert he should get to notice.

#

Devon said I could decorate his new apartment however I wanted, as long as it didn't cost too much. The more I did to it, the more it felt like it was my home, too. Living with Devon full-time would be amazing. I'd slept over every Friday and Saturday night since he moved in.

When I came home that first Sunday afternoon, after being at Devon's Friday and Saturday night, I was anxious about what Ree would do. I'd hoped she'd be out with Allen, the guy she'd been with when I brought Olivia over. But nope, she was home alone, lounging across the front seats of the van, wrapped up in a blanket, though it was warm inside from the coffee can candles.

She looked up from the book she was reading, which was *Madame Bovary*. She'd already read the ones that were more her thing, from our last thrift shop haul. She raised her eyebrows and gave me a long look, which somehow turned my nervousness into anger.

I said, "How do you like it?" That was to remind her of all the times she'd run off on me.

She rolled her eyes and went back to reading her book.

Ree and I were supposed to move in with Allen soon. He was renting a room in somebody else's house and still had to wait a couple more weeks for the two-bedroom apartment he was getting for the three of us. I felt kind of bad, thinking maybe they should get a one-bedroom, because I wasn't sure I'd be going with them.

But either way, this had been a long bout of time free, maybe our longest yet. I couldn't wait to end it.

#

On a Saturday night, Devon's was watching TV after the dinner I fixed, scrambled eggs with sausage, buttered toast and orange slices. I loved acting like I was Devon's wife and like this was our place together. Even sweeping the floor, making the bed or washing the dishes seemed sexy here. Last weekend, I'd tried to cook scrambled eggs in the microwave and they were too rubbery to eat. But this time, I cooked them in a pan on the stove and they were good. I felt like that erased my earlier mistake.

I'd finally collected enough letter "M" wall décor. I was ready to hang it on the wall above Devon's bed, which doubled as the couch. He'd said I was driving him crazy, when I made him drive me all over town looking for the letter M. He said he felt like he was on Sesame Street or something. But he smiled whenever he said it, so I think he was really glad I wanted to make a home with him and put his initial on the wall. I had seven of them, in different sizes, made of wood and metal.

I felt dreamily wifely now, on a full stomach and on my second beer, figuring out the M arrangement on the floor.

I hoped Miller would be my last name someday, too. Also, I was glad his last name started with such a nicely shaped, symmetrical letter. The letters G, J or P, for example, wouldn't look nearly as good on the wall, and it could get even worse than that. Like, an O would just look like a bunch of zeroes and an X would just look crazy. If anybody's last name even started with an X. Bit by bit, Devon and I were putting together a real home.

It was so cool watching him put the letters up on the wall, under my instructions. Very manly, husbandly, holding nails between his lips. I sipped my beer and watched his bicep bulge when he lifted the hammer. I was trying to get myself in the right frame of mind for what was to come.

I didn't make any promises to Devon about it. That turned out to be good because I'd planned to go all the way with him every weekend for the past month and chickened out every time. But tonight was the night. I didn't want to lose him.

I admired his handiwork, after the letters were up on the wall. Even though it was really more my handiwork, I guess. I asked him to put some music on and light the candles, while I got us another round of beers. I guzzled half of mine, behind the refrigerator door.

I sat on his lap on the couch/bed and let things take their natural course. But when we'd progressed to the point where I usually finished him off in my mouth, I invited him in down there, instead.

"Are you sure, babe?" he said, searching my face, wanting to be sure he wasn't being a jerk or anything, I guess.

"I'm sure, babe," I said. In my mind, I was already counting backwards from 1,000, like I'd always done when something hurt or when I thought it was going to hurt. Like when I got my ears pierced back in Roswell.

Then he got off the bed. What the hell. It took so much for me to get my nerve up and we'd been right there. Now

I'd have to get my nerve up all over again. I was about to tell him to just forget it.

He came back with a condom and rolled it on. That took me even further out of the mood, realizing how stupid I'd been to not even think about protection. But, enough of this. It just had to be done.

I said, "Hold on a sec, babe." I got up and picked up my beer, and started guzzling the last half of it.

Devon looked sad. He said, "Hey, it's okay. You don't have to, you know."

"No, it's all right. I want to. Go ahead," I said, getting back into position underneath him. I started my mental countdown again. *1,000, 999, 998, 997...*

It hurt. A burning feeling started at number 987. It eased up some after a couple of strokes.

By 920, it was over.

"Are you okay, babe?" he said.

"Sure, babe."

"Well? How was it?"

"It was good."

"Next time will be better," he said, removing the condom.

I didn't care how it was or how it would be. The important thing was that it was done. The big, impossible scary problem in my mind was over. And now I'd be able to keep this almost grown man in my life. That's what I cared about. *I did it. I did it. I did it!*

Devon kept cuddling with me. Then he wanted to screw again. But I sort of demanded that he get up and take me to the Taco Bell drive-through instead. I deserved Taco Bell.

He kind of groaned but he got up and got dressed. We bundled up for the cold and took a late night drive under the beautiful dark sky with its big, big stars. I thought of that

Van Gogh painting with its giant yellow stars in the crazy, swirly sky.

I made Devon order me a dozen hard tacos and ate half of them on the way home. I didn't realize I was that hungry. Oh my god, the juicy, seasoned filling, the shredded melty cheese, the hot and crispy shells. They were delicious beyond description.

Devon said, "Now you're gonna moan like that. Now?"

#

It was a cold December day but at least it wasn't windy. Ree and I huddled around the fire at our campsite. We had tossed some whole potatoes on the grill. That's all, because neither of us felt like walking to the grocery store.

Ree went into the van and came out with two cups of her kitchen wine. I really needed it right then because I was about to clear the other big hurdle in my life. Clearing one of my two hurdles, having sex with Devon, gave me confidence to keep on going. Dirty jokes wanted to pop up in my mind about that because clearing a hurdle wasn't really accurate. Successful pole vaulting? Winning a pogo-stick competition? Oh god. Now I sounded like Devon and Raul.

"You think this is funny?" Ree had that sour look on her face.

"No. I wasn't even thinking about the van and all that. But, you know, it's not my fault."

"What's not your fault?" Ree set her wine down and lit her pipe. For the first time, I noticed little wrinkles at the sides of her eyes, a little grey in her hair, visible now that the black rinse had worn off. She looked smaller or something and I felt a little sorry for her. But only a little.

I said, "Well. It's not my fault that the van died, for one thing. If it really needs to be stated." The van wouldn't start and after Allen tried a couple of different fixes, he'd declared it deceased. Like Allen said, we shouldn't really be surprised. I mean, it had been around longer than I had. We'd put a lot of miles on it, too.

She said, "It's not your fault but it's also not like you didn't use any of it up, either."

Ree seemed to keep count of every little thing I used lately, especially when she was mad. Well, good. She should like the news I was about to give her then. I guess I'd done all that worrying about it for nothing. She wouldn't have to count up everything I cost her to stay alive any more.

I said, "Yeah, sorry for living. It's also not my fault that Allen dumped you." She winced and I wished I'd said something softer, like "left you" instead of "dumped you," at least." I tossed another log on the fire. I moved my lawn chair closer to the flames, sipped Ree's sour, awful wine that she seemed so proud of. I sort of went into a trance, watching the dancing, popping orange and yellow fire on the brown and grey wood. Fire could easily put you into a trance.

She said, "Alpaca face."

"Huh?"

"Allen Alpaca face."

"Oh. I thought you were talking about me." He kind of did have an alpaca face, come to think of it. Big, dark, googly eyes, and that weird puff of hair on top, in front of the big bald spot.

"Alkie Allen, Allen Alien, Alopecia head," I said, trying to get in the spirit of it.

She didn't respond to it, though and I wondered why I even tried to be friendly with her. She said, "That last fight was over you, you know. So, with the van, and with Allen too, you played your part. You didn't have to flirt with him. Waltz around in front of him. All that."

I'd be less hurt if she'd punched me in the mouth. "Flirting? With Allen? Oh my god. It's not my fault that he's a pig. By the way, thanks for bringing a pig like that around in the first place. I truly appreciate having to deal with that. But you never even thought of that, did you."

She got quiet then and we both just sipped our wine and watched the fire dance, waiting for the tension to pass. I didn't want to tell her I wanted to go live with Devon right now. I didn't want to leave like this.

She made the choice for me. After a while, she stood up and made motions like she was dusting herself off, clearing herself of me, I guess. She said, "Well kid, we're about done. This has been coming on for a while now. There's nothing more I can do for you now that you can't do just as well for yourself."

She went back in the van and rummaged around, while I stayed by the fire like I was frozen in place there.

She came back out with her big travel bag, stuffed full. She sort of mumbled, not looking at me, "They don't tell you, but it's always like this. The mother of the species always has to be the one to leave. The damn kids will hang on and drain you forever, if you let them."

When I could bear to look up at her, what I saw through my tears was… nothing. She was already gone. She didn't even say good-bye. She just left me with that one last complaint to remember her by.

I stood and walked to the back side of the campsite.
Ree's coyote call floated back to me, through the icy air.
Ruh-ray-ooo yip, yip.

Off in the distance, a large reddish coyote dashed into the
pines.

#

It was a lazy July afternoon in Santa Fe and Olivia and I
lounged by the sparkling turquoise swimming pool,
slathered in sunscreen. We each had a plastic tumbler filled
with diet Sprite and vodka on ice, heavy on the vodka. A
fast, bouncy song I couldn't make out the words to played
on my phone, a bit tinny through my cheapo miniature
speaker. It was only us two, in loungers under umbrellas,
and two small boys on the other side of the pool, with what
looked to be their older sister or a babysitter.

We sipped our drinks and watched the kids splash and
run around, through our matching pairs of sunglasses. I
lifted my sunglasses up to admire the pedicures we'd gotten
together the day before. Olivia had orange sherbet-colored
toenails with a tiny flower painted on each big toe and mine
were hot pink, with two tiny hearts. Having a best friend
again was fantastic.

Watching one little boy dunk the other one, Olivia said,
"You ever want kids?"

"Hell no," I blurted, making her laugh.

"Gosh, they're not *that* bad, are they? Well, those two
over there do seem pretty bratty but I mean in general."

"Eh. I don't know. I really never liked the idea of it, to
be honest. They're cute and everything, I guess, but they
just seem like a real heavy load. You'd be weighed down

big time, for a long time. Trapped. You know? Plus, can you even imagine pushing one of those watermelons out?"

Olivia said, "Well, ahem. I believe I might be doing more than just imagining it."

"What? You're pregnant? No! Are you?"

"Yes! Yes, I am."

"Wow. Uh, sorry about that stuff I just said. I only meant it about myself, you know. And I'm just weird. So, this is good news, then?"

Olivia said, "It is. It's not like we planned it or anything. But I have to admit, I am excited about it now. I went and got a test this morning, so I just found out for sure. And I think we're ready. I mean, I'm eighteen now and Raul is twenty, and he's making good money. We're ready enough, anyway."

"So, Raul doesn't know yet, then?"

"Not yet. I want to wait and tell him in person tonight. He knows I'm late with Aunt Flo, though."

"Wow. Well, congratulations!" I held up my drink and we toasted.

"Thanks. Guess I better drink up while I can," she said, taking a sip of vodka and Sprite.

I was about to say something about that but then I just took a glug too, hoping to slow my brain bees. Olivia having a baby would change things. I hoped she'd still have time for me, then. Why the hell couldn't anything just stay the same for a while, whenever I got things the way I liked them?

Once in a while, a change did turn out to be better but you'd only find that out later on. Like us four moving down here to Santa Fe, for example. At the time, I was a wreck. I'd barely even got settled into Devon's apartment before he lost his job in Taos. His boss let Raul go, too. There just wasn't enough construction or home improvement work in December, especially in such a small town.

Olivia's brother-in-law was a general contractor here, and the next thing I knew, the guys had job offers from him, at close to twice the money they'd made in Taos. Raul and Olivia got an apartment in this snazzy complex here and we stayed with them for a while. Then somebody signed for Devon and me to get an apartment of our own, in the next building over from Olivia and Raul. I could hardly believe it at first. Sometimes I still wandered around in awe, admiring the cool-to-the-touch stone countertops and gleaming stainless steel appliances, the washer and dryer just for us, the covered balcony. The place was high end and it practically looked brand new.

That was one good thing about Devon working with construction guys. Whether it was signing a lease, buying booze or gummies or even the vape Devon had got me as one of my Christmas presents, somebody who was of legal age would always help him out. It came with a price, though, that brotherhood thing. If one of the guys asked for a favor, Devon said we kinda had to help them, too. Like last month, I had to watch this little girl for three days, the daughter of one of Devon's work buddies. She couldn't go to her regular daycare because she was sick. And neither of her parents wanted to miss work. Then I caught whatever ick the kid had and passed it on to Devon, too.

Olivia cut into my sprint down memory lane. She said, "Want to grill, when the guys get home? I have some ground beef for burgers thawing out in the fridge. Do you have bread? It's too hot to go to the store." The four of us grilled out here a lot together, ever since the weather had warmed up. There were two grills and a big covered patio, over on the far side of the pool. Plus, there were tables and chairs and a bar with a sink and small refrigerator. There was even a big TV.

I said, "Yeah, I have a whole loaf of bread. We just went grocery shopping last night, so I have stuff for the side dishes, too. Let's see, I have a jar of chunky applesauce and a couple of cans of pork and beans. I could probably do a raw fruit and veggie platter, too."

Olivia nodded. She and I joked about how we'd become like middle-aged housewives. I didn't know about her but I loved my homemaking routine: food preparation, cleaning and laundry in the morning, while I watched TV. And I'd hang out with Olivia most afternoons. Then we had our nights with the guys, when they got home from work. Not to mention getting to live in a beautiful, comfortable place. Yep, being a boring old housewife at fifteen years old was paradise to me.

I thought of Ree calling me a soccer mom and a Suzy homemaker, and felt a pang in my chest. I'd let Ree make fun my domestic livestock ways all she wanted, if I could just know that she was all right and that she didn't hate me. She didn't answer my calls.

I forced my mind back to the present. I tried to stay in the here and now as much as I could, when it was a happy place to be, which it really was these days. That was Devon's approach to life. He thought it was wrong, morally even, to dwell on bad things in the past, when you had a good life at the moment. That it wasn't being grateful for what you had. He made sense. Whenever I caught myself feeling sick about Ree, I'd remember what he said, that I was thinking in an ungrateful way and needed to stop. It worked.

I remembered Olivia's pregnancy. I said, "Oh, wait. If you're going to give Raul the big news, should we wait and grill tomorrow night instead?" It seemed like a pretty private and special occasion to me. One they might want to be alone for.

"Oh, gosh. I didn't even think of that. Yeah. We'll grill tomorrow night, then. Okay?"

"Sure. Uh-oh. Look who's coming."

Olivia sat up, so she could look around better. "Oh my god. Hey, let's grill after all, if she sticks around. Please don't leave me alone with the Gi-na." She pronounced it like the last two syllables of "vagina."

"Okay. I won't." Olivia's sister Regina was twenty-four, which meant she could get us booze, tobacco and weed. She could but she wouldn't. She wasn't the cool type of big sister. She was the mother type of big sister, who felt free to give unsolicited advice and scold Olivia whenever she felt like it, and who always thought she knew best. Our guys worked for Regina's husband too, which gave her extra leverage.

I kind of liked Regina anyway but I wouldn't dare say that to Olivia. Regina didn't seem to me like she was trying to be nasty, but like she actually cared and wanted to help. She just didn't understand teenage girls like us, who didn't go to school and lived with our boyfriends. We felt like we'd pretty much earned adult status and should be treated accordingly. Regina didn't bother me that much but she drove Olivia nuts.

"Hey there, kiddos. What's up?" Regina said. *Kiddos*. She showed her perception of us right away.

Olivia tensed up. "Hi," she muttered.

"Livy. Is that a salon pedi I see on your feet?"

It got uncomfortable when Olivia didn't answer. I answered for her, to break the tension. "Yeah. We both did.

We went to that place called 'Nailed It.'" I held out my feet and wiggled my toes, in their flip-flops, for emphasis.

"Hmm. Two girls without jobs have money for salon pedicures. You ladies must be independently wealthy."

If you didn't argue with Regina, she usually moved on to a different topic right away. I noticed this the first time I met her. I'd tried to tell Olivia.

Olivia said, "Sorry, Gi-na." The few times I'd seen these two together, Olivia would immediately seem to lose a decade off her age. She'd start acting very sulky and childish. Which then kind of made it seem like she needed the Gi-na's guidance.

Regina said, "Hmm. All right then, smarty."

After finishing her alcoholic beverage in one gulp, Olivia re-positioned her lounger so she lay flat on her back. She closed her eyes. She stuck her bottom lip out, like a pouting toddler. I stifled the urge to crack up laughing.

Regina said, "Hmm. And what's that you're drinking there, and in the middle of the day, no less?"

"Sprite," Olivia said, sulkily.

Regina said, "Well, I hope that's all. Remember, you can't drink with your meds. Don't forget what happened last time. Anyway. I just came by to tell you girls that it's time to register for Fall classes at the community college, if you're interested. I was driving by there today and thought of you two. You can go online to see what courses they offer. Livy, there's a nurse's aide course I thought you might like. Let me know if you guys need any help."

"That's a good idea. Thanks for thinking of us," I said, though of course I wasn't old enough to get in. Olivia knew my real age now but Regina didn't. Olivia continued to act like she was asleep. She added a snore for good measure and I had to fake a cough.

Regina said, "Oh, I also have some good news. Guess what?"

She answered before I could guess.

"I'm expecting!"

Olivia, suddenly wide awake, bolted straight up in her lounger. "Expecting what?"

"Um, a baby?" Regina said, looking confused at the challenge in Olivia's question.

"Well, that figures. Congratulations," Olivia said, in a quite non-congratulatory tone. She flopped down on her back again, then cursed when the back of her head hit the hard plastic lounger.

Regina said, "We've been trying for a while so we're very pleased. Very blessed."

"Well, congratulations! That's great," I said.

She nodded at me, then turned back to Olivia's inert form. "Well, okay, I see how it's going to be today. Guess I'll be on my way, then. Livy, Mother wants you to come for Sunday dinner. She's very hurt that you hardly ever show up for her Sunday dinners anymore."

Olivia pursed her lips but kept her eyes closed and didn't say anything else until Regina left.

Then I got an earful about Regina, again. Apparently, Olivia thought her pregnancy was a chance to even the score with Regina, to reach a big life milestone first, for once. But then Regina's announcement had ruined everything. Regina was pregnant first and would probably have her baby first. And Regina co-owned a successful general contracting business with her husband. She also had a husband, in the first place. Regina also had a house that they were buying, not renting and blah, blah, blah.

Olivia was sure that the Gi-na's pregnancy would be the important and celebrated pregnancy now, to the rest of her family. In comparison, unmarried Olivia's slightly less far along pregnancy would just seem shabby now. Olivia's pregnancy was not nearly as good as the Gi-na's pregnancy.

I cut into her rant to ask what meds she was on, the ones Regina had mentioned. "Not to be nosy but are you sure whatever meds you're on are okay to be taking, with a baby on the way now?" It seemed like every medicine I'd ever taken had some big warning on its label about taking it during pregnancy. Not that the booze was good, either but Olivia already knew that.

She said, "Oh, no. That was just some allergy medication. I don't need it now."

"Oh. You mean like seasonal allergies?" I remembered the term from TV commercials.

"Uh-huh. Anyway, that goddamned Gi-na..."

It grated on me, having to play along instead of being real. It wasn't Regina's fault that she had her act together better than Olivia did. It was weird that Olivia always tried to be on the same level with someone that much older than her, anyway. Even a normal barely-eighteen-year-old shouldn't expect to be as advanced in life as a twenty-four-year-old. But Olivia would probably ditch me if I seemed to be sticking up for the Gi-na.

Nobody's perfect though and Olivia was still a super best friend. Even better than Juno, especially when you considered that whole dead body thing Juno dragged me into. Most days, it didn't make any difference to me that I didn't agree with some of Olivia's ideas. It was her life, after all. But right then, it was just hitting me wrong and she was ruining my vodka buzz. I was relieved when she decided she and Raul would eat dinner alone after all, since Regina had left.

#

Olivia's pregnancy made her tired and sick, so she stayed home in bed a lot. I missed hanging out with her every day. Her pregnancy was changing everything already. But thanks to Regina's idea, I went on the community college website just for kicks and found a late summer, not-for-credit interior design class. So that kept me pretty busy.

You needed an ID even to sign up for a non-credit class, though. In the end, Devon signed me up under his name and I attended the class as Devon Isaac Miller. I wore Devon's work shirts to class, with no make-up, trying to look like a girl who would go by a guy's name.

We students all had to buy a big, tri-fold poster board for the class. We attached paint, fabric and wallpaper swatches onto it, ideas for our overall décor plans for our homes. I went with the eclectic style because I couldn't afford to throw out what we already had and start over again. Of course, I was also limited since we were just renting but I'd file away the ideas I couldn't use now for the day when we finally did own a place.

I'd also had to start figuring out the bus system to get to my class, so now I could get out and about on my own more, too. And I met an elderly woman named Celia by the pool one day, when I was there without Olivia. She hired me to clean her apartment every week. So I had some spending money of my own now and didn't have to ask Devon for every little thing I wanted anymore.

I was super glad because sometimes he'd criticize me about money and it got on my nerves. Like when I only used the vape he bought me a couple of times. That pissed me off, because it was supposed to be a Christmas gift, for one thing. You weren't supposed to throw a present in someone's face. Besides, how could I have known if I'd like vaping or not before I even had a chance to try it? Shoot me for liking the old kind of cigarettes better. Shoot me twice for not even smoking that much anyway. If he brought it up again, now I could give him back the money he paid for the stupid vape and tell him where to stick it.

That was just a dumb argument we'd had a couple of times, though. Overall, it was a very happy and exciting time in my life, aside from the one big, constant ache, Ree's refusal to return my calls.

Sometimes I thought it might be more than a coincidence when I saw that coyote, right after Ree did her coyote call, at the campsite in Taos. I'd remember it as I was dropping off to sleep and it would wake me all the way up all over again. But then in the light of day, it would seem insane, to even suspect for one second that Ree could have changed herself into a coyote. Olivia thought it might be possible. She believed in such things, she said. I didn't even bother telling Devon about it.

#

One night, Devon didn't come home for dinner. He'd had to work late before, but he always called. After an hour went by, I called him but my call went to voicemail. I ate my half of the spaghetti and green beans I'd fixed and put his in the fridge. Eating without him was meant as a small punishment, I guess.

I didn't call him again until another hour went by, not until 8:00 p.m. I remembered him and Raul laughing about some guy's crazy girlfriend blowing up the guy's phone when they were on a job one time. I sure didn't want to be that girl. But when he didn't answer me that time either, I started getting real upset and I saw that girl's side of things. I called Olivia, who said that Raul had come home on time and no, they didn't know where Devon was.

He finally came stumbling in, drunk, after midnight. We got in a big argument about that, of course. Then he started yelling about what the hell did I want from him, that he was too young for this shit and that there was no ring on his finger, anyway.

I was too stunned to reply. I cried in the bathroom, behind the locked door, fist in mouth. If that's how he felt then I wouldn't give him the pleasure of thinking I cared anymore, either.

He was asleep when I finally came out. He was splashed diagonally across the bed, with his work boots still on. I grabbed a pillow off the bed and a bath towel to use as a blanket. I ate a piece of plain bread to help settle my nervous stomach, then slept on the couch.

Things went back to normal for a while after that. It was like the whole topic was too dangerous to poke at. It could blow us apart.

A month later, he did it again. Only this time, he didn't come home until the sun was up the next morning. He looked like hell warmed over and begged me in a whisper to please, please just let him sleep, that he was too miserably hungover to fight. I got him some ibuprofen and ice water, then shut the bedroom blinds and softly closed the bedroom door behind me. I surrendered.

It was obvious now. We'd gone wooden, as far as he was concerned. I loved the wooden life myself, being domestic livestock and everything. But I knew better than anybody that some people just couldn't stand a steady, everyday type relationship. Talk about not being grateful for what you had. I started to feel almost like Devon had died. It was very sad.

Later that night, he felt better. He begged me to forgive him. He cried. It was kind of icky but fascinating in a weird way, too. It reminded me of a TV series on abnormal psychology that I'd watched somewhere that Ree and I stayed. It was at that old Bill guy's house, Bill the Pill. I think it was in Grants, where something really bad happened to me with Bill's grown-up devil son that I don't like thinking about. That's another thing. When something really bad happens to you, it connects in your mind with other really bad things that have happened to you before. And then, if you don't watch it, you're a basket case.

So, it seemed like Devon was trying to bring back the fireworks we had at first but it could only be that exciting in a bad way now, because we could never be a brand new couple again. Him being so mean to me, then crying and practically kissing my feet. Then doing it again was like a rollercoaster or fireworks instead of steady, calm days. Or maybe that wasn't exactly right but whatever it was, I couldn't stand it.

After Devon calmed down, he decided we ought to call Olivia and Raul and have them meet us by the pool. We could grill and take a dip in the water, like old times, he said. *Like old times, when we were new and exciting together.* I felt like he didn't know what he was doing but that I did. He just said we might not have many more pool days left this year. He should have said we might not have many more days left together at all.

He called Raul and then the guys handed their phones to Olivia and me, so we could figure out the food. She was feeling better, she said. It seemed the worst of her early pregnancy symptoms, the extreme tiredness and morning sickness, were over now. Her symptoms had been far worse than the Gi-na's, she said. She seemed pleased to inform me that the Gi-na had no idea what serious first trimester symptoms were like.

I thawed a pack of pork chops in the microwave and emptied some canned pineapple rings into a bowl. Outdoors, we grilled, we ate, we swam and talked. Olivia looked all around her but somehow didn't notice that I was looking right at her when she snuck a big pour of vodka into her tumbler of Sprite. I felt at a strange distance from that and everything else, almost like it was a scene I wasn't really part of but was only watching on the big outdoor TV.

#

"Where the hell are you?" It was Olivia on the phone. I hadn't picked up the other times she called. I'd wanted to let everything die down a little first.

I said, "Well, hello to you, too."

"Why didn't you answer my calls? What in the world are you doing?"

I said, "Don't worry. I'm right here. I'm looking at your apartment building through my window now."

"You came home? Wait. You can't see my apartment building from inside your place."

"No, silly sausage. I'm at Celia's." I was fixing lasagna and mixed vegetables, to portion into frozen dinners for Celia. I took my chance to leave Devon three weeks earlier, after I found out Celia was going to Europe for a month with her daughter. Celia was so old that her daughter was retired, too. She'd asked me to check on her two chi-weenie dogs twice a day while she was gone. I said I couldn't commit to it because I was trying to leave my boyfriend and didn't know if I'd be around.

So then we worked out a deal where I'd live here for the month and take care of her dogs. She'd also found some other chores I could do for extra money while I was here, though a free place and food for the month was payment enough. She was a nice lady.

Olivia said, "Celia? That old woman you clean for?"

"Yep. She's out of town and I'm staying here while I figure out where to go next. Don't tell Devon, though."

"You know I won't. But he came by here looking for you. He looked like he hadn't slept and his eyes were red, like he'd been crying."

"Well, that's good, at least."

She laughed. "Remind me to never piss you off. You're meaner than shit."

I felt a bit proud. "Hold on a sec. I've got to take something out of the oven." I took the lasagna out and set it on the stovetop to cool.

I said, "Are you still there?"

"I am still here. When does Celia get back?"

"In about a week. Why?"

There was a long pause. "Olivia?" I said.

"Um, can I come over?"

Celia hadn't said if I could have guests over or not. But it was only Olivia. "Sure," I said. She took a long time to arrive. The lasagna had cooled enough to portion into Celia's single meal-sized freezer containers. So had the vegetables. I had a dozen meals labeled and stacked in the freezer before the chi-weenies went into a barking frenzy over the knock at the door.

"Chia! Chai! Hush up!" I don't know why I even bothered yelling at the dogs anymore. They only obeyed Celia.

I opened the door. There stood Olivia, with several bags full of stuff at her feet.

I moved aside and stood there while she hauled all her stuff in. I said, "Um, what are you doing?"

Olivia said, "Well, hello to you, too."

I laughed, remembering that's what I said to her on the phone earlier. "Hello. Now, what the hell do you think you're doing?"

She flopped down on one of Celia's chairs, the one that was upholstered in a purple-blue iris print. She said, "I've left Raul the fool."

"No! What happened? It seemed like you two were doing great together."

"Not at all. Not anymore. I'm tired of how distrusting he is, for one thing. He didn't even believe that I was pregnant."

"What on earth. Why not?"

"Well, oh gosh… Do you promise not to judge?"

I don't know why people even talk about not judging. Of course I'd judge, if she, or anyone else, did something stupid or wrong, for example. Who wouldn't? "Okay, sure," I said. I wanted to know what was going on.

"All right, then. Here goes. But remember, you promised."

I sat down too, since it seemed like it was going to be a while before she gave up the chisme caliente. My chair was upholstered in a red-orange poppy print. I wasn't sure about Celia's taste in décor. Her place looked kind of expensive but it was just too floral for me. I guess she didn't take a class like I did, so she didn't know that floral was not a recognized style of décor.

Olivia said, "Okey-dokey, then. Confession time. Drumroll, please."

She sat there looking at me. Then it dawned on me that she wanted a drumroll, literally. I grabbed a pot and a spoon from the kitchen and thwapped the spoon on the pot a few times. She nodded, so I guess it was close enough.

"I wasn't pregnant," she said.

"Huh? The test was wrong?"

"Not exactly." She dipped into the bowl of potpourri on Celia's coffee table, scooped out a handful and brought it up towards her mouth.

"Don't eat that!" I said. Olivia looked up in surprise. Damn. Even the dogs knew not to eat the potpourri.

She said, "I was, um, just smelling it. Gosh." She'd opened her mouth already, though. She was totally going to eat it.

Then it dawned on me. "Oh, no. You had a miscarriage. I'm so sorry."

Olivia sighed, like I was the one who was making this into an annoying guessing game. She said, "I never was pregnant, okay? I made it up. There now see? That's how much I trust you. I didn't have to tell you that."

"Um, thank you for trusting me? I'm still confused, though. You don't like how Raul didn't believe that you were pregnant. But… you weren't pregnant?"

"Right, because that's a completely different issue. He didn't know I wasn't pregnant until I told him I wasn't pregnant. So, either way, he doesn't trust me."

"But---"

"Trust is very important to me," she said, in a tone like she wasn't messing around.

"Okay. Got it," I said. I stopped myself from asking why she made up the pregnancy. I figured whatever she said wouldn't make sense anyway. I already knew there was something a little off about Olivia. Raul had probably overlooked it because she was so pretty, with her blonde hair and green eyes. I overlooked it because it didn't make that much difference to me anyway. But I guess she didn't really need a reason to leave Raul anyway. Just wanting to was reason enough.

She said, "How much longer are we staying here?"

We? I said, "Um, I can't really let you stay here. I don't have Celia's permission."

She made a face. "Permission, really?" she said, like permission was a ridiculous concept.

I considered it from all angles. Olivia was my best friend, whereas I'd probably never see Celia again after she came back from her trip. And Celia hadn't said I couldn't have anybody else stay over with me. Also, it wasn't like Olivia was the type to damage the place or anything.

She said, "Well, I can't go back now. Raul will be home from work. Then I'd have to explain why I took all my stuff out of the apartment. *Please* don't make me go to the Gina."

I decided that if Celia somehow caught me, I'd say I wanted someone else here because I got scared. I'd say someone jiggled the door knob or something. "Oh, all right. But you can't stay more than five days, just in case she comes home early. And Raul the tool absolutely, one hundred percent cannot know. He'll tell Deviance and I just don't have the energy for any more of his bullshit."

Olivia bounced up and down on her chair in victory. "It's Raul the fool," she said.

#

I was glad Olivia was with me, after my time at Celia's was over. Olivia was from here, so she knew a lot of people.

Right now, we were staying with someone Olivia knew from the neighborhood she'd grown up in. Melinda was Regina's age but she seemed kind of mentally slow.

Melinda didn't work. She lived on some kind of government check. I felt kind of bad, like maybe we were pushing ourselves on her. But I saw Olivia's point of view about it, too. She was talking about how we actually made Melinda's life better.

Melinda had gone out somewhere. Olivia and I took the opportunity to discuss her, while drinking ice tea until we were goggle-eyed, watching some boring daytime shows on TV and making stuff at the kitchen table.

Olivia, Melinda and I had pooled our money for fabric, thread and the other supplies we needed. We were making flattish, palm-sized Zozobra dolls, keepsakes to sell at the big celebration that was coming up. Olivia said it was a big deal in Santa Fe. Every year, they'd burn a fifty-foot tall Zozobra effigy. It stood for burning away everyone's worries and starting over fresh. It seemed to me that it would make more sense for New Year's Eve but nope, it was at the end of August. I'd told Olivia about the stuff Ree used to make and sell to tourists, and then we came up with this idea. If it went well, we'd branch out and try to sell other items.

She said, "See, I don't think Melinda really has any friends, for one thing. She only has her mom. I mean, don't you think that's kind of sad?"

As one who had often had only my mother and wished for friends, I agreed. It was sad.

She said, "And look, we include her in everything we do, don't we? All week long, we've cooked and ate with her, watched TV with her, even included her in this chance to make some money, right? Ouch! Dammit." Olivia had stuck herself with the needle she was sewing up a miniature Zozobra with.

"Hold on. Don't get blood on the doll." I rushed to the counter for a paper towel.

"Thanks."

I said, "You're welcome. I wish Zozobra was cuter. These dolls look purely evil."

"I know, right? Anyway, if it will make you feel better, I guess we could clean the place when we finish up with this for the day. But Melinda likes having us here. I'd know it if she didn't. And, not to be rude or anything but, you know, it's not like she's paying for this place, anyway."

I didn't know what to say to that last part so I didn't say anything. I smoothed the batting on the doll I was working on, so it was kind of evenly puffed up instead of flat, then dropped it in the box and started making another one.

Melinda had a one-bedroom apartment in a ratty part of town. Sleeping on her couch was a big step down from the beautiful apartment I'd had with Devon. But it was also a big step up from time free with Ree, camping out in the van or a shack or a cave.

But if I had a choice, I'd still pick time free with Ree anywhere, over not having Ree in my life at all.

After we had a dozen finished dolls, we decided that was enough for one day. I cleaned the bathroom while Olivia dusted and swept. Then I took the trash to the dumpster while Olivia started on dinner. When I came back, she was standing at the counter, shaking her head over the skimpy assortment of ingredients spread out in front of her: Two eggs, an onion and half a bag of dried pinto beans.

She said, "What the hell am I supposed to do with this?"

"Hmm. I guess we just cook it all up together. Do you want to start the beans or chop the onion?"

She said, "Beans."

"Dammit." We both hated chopping onions. They made our eyes water.

Olivia filled a bowl with water. "I can cook the beans in the microwave, right? Otherwise, they'll take too damn long. Dried beans take forever anyway."

"Yeah. I don't see why you can't microwave them."

"Well, I don't know what the hell we're gonna do for food tomorrow. Do you know what day of the month Melinda gets more money on her food card?"

I said, "Nope. Guess we'll just have to put you back on your favorite street corner again."

That made us both laugh. She said, "Might have to, if we don't figure out some other kind of trick pretty soon."

"Yep. Guess we spent too much on the Zozobra stuff."

"Just don't make me ask the Gi-na for help. That is all I ask."

I said, "I would never make you ask the Gi-na for help. Hey, did Melinda say where she was going? She's been gone a while now."

"Um, if she did, I don't remember."

The beans did take a long time. We finally settled for eating them when they were still crunchy. We'd just put a plate in the fridge for Melinda and sat down at the table with our beans with onion, egg and ketchup, when somebody burst in like there was some big emergency.

"Oh, hi Mrs. Baker," Olivia said to the large woman who stood glowering in front of us, with her hands on her hips.

When Mrs. Baker didn't answer, Olivia introduced me to her, as if the woman didn't look homicidal. "Mrs. Baker, this is Star Garza. She's a friend of mine, and Melinda's friend now, too. By the way, have you seen Melinda? We just put her dinner in the refrigerator."

The woman, who I figured must be Melinda's mother, still didn't speak or move. I found myself feeling around in my back pocket for my knife. That's where I kept it in the summer, when I wore flip-flops and didn't have socks and shoes to stash it in.

Finally, Mrs. Baker cleared her throat. She said, "When you two are through eating, you'll have to pack up and leave."

Then she turned and walked out.

We just sat there for a second, then Olivia shrugged and tasted the food on her plate. "It's not bad," she said about the food, ignoring the thing with Melinda's mother.

I wasn't going to let her off quite that easy. I said, "I guess I was right, after all. Melinda didn't want us here."

Olivia said, "Wish I'd known that before we cleaned the place."

We finished our dinner without talking, then quietly packed up.

We spent the night in Olivia's old Toyota Corolla.

At one point, she poked me in the ribs until I woke up and asked her what the hell her problem was. I was sleeping next to her in the front seat, with both seats back as far as they'd go.

She said, "I'm scared."

For some reason, it struck me as hilarious. Then my laughing made her laugh. And then we went back to sleep.

#

Olivia and I didn't get to sell our dolls at Zozobra. We didn't make it until the end of August when the festival was set to happen. The week after we got kicked out of Melinda's place, we slept in Olivia's car, then in the restroom at a public park. After that, we stayed at an apartment where an old boyfriend of hers lived with his roommate, who she also knew from school.

The two guys, Zach and Peter, got takeout pizza and the four of us were sitting around eating it, drinking beer and binge watching a reality show about life in prison. The guys were nice. Zach, the one Olivia used to date, moved into the other guy's bedroom, so we girls could have a bedroom of our own while we were there.

Nobody seemed to be trying to put the moves on anybody, which led Olivia and me to wonder if Zach and Peter were secretly gay. Either way, a comfortable bed, a bathtub, a fridge full of food and all those other everyday luxuries made me practically giddy.. The guys were good company, too. I was in an especially good frame of mind right then and Olivia seemed to be, too. So I couldn't make any sense out of what happened next.

Olivia said she didn't feel good and that she thought she'd go to bed early. Zach, Peter and I said goodnight to her, then went back to watching TV. *Cops* was on now.

Maybe twenty minutes later, during a commercial, I noticed that I didn't have my phone. I'd left it in the bedroom I shared with Olivia, which gave me a small panic. I liked to keep it with me, on the off chance that Ree would call. I still hoped she might miss me sometime, like I missed her. Or who knew, maybe she'd even have some kind of emergency and need my help. I knew it wasn't likely but what if she called once and I wasn't there? That one chance to make up with her might be it. She might never call again.

I tiptoed into our bedroom and, in the light from the hallway, I saw an economy-sized bottle of Tylenol lying on my side of the bed, with Tylenol tablets spilled all over the bedcovers. It just didn't look right. I switched on the lights, and said, "Olivia? Olivia, are you okay?" I patted her, then shook her, then yelled for help.

The guys came running in. They seemed to read the situation from the spilled pills and my shrieking and shaking Olivia.

"Olivia? O-liv-i-a!" Finally, she stirred enough to mumble something.

"Did you take some Tylenol?" I shouted. "How many Tylenols did you take?"

Zach called 9-1-1. After giving the required details, he said to me, "She says to put her on her side. Then point her nose down towards the bed."

Peter was already there, helping me turn her. "That's so she won't choke, if she vomits," he said.

Zach said, "I'm going to wait outside, to help them find the place."

The medics were there right away. They took Olivia away on a stretcher. Zach went with them.

Then, suddenly, all was quiet, except for the TV, vaguely, from the other room. Peter and I sat down on the bed for a second, like we were both still trying to get a grip on what had just happened.

"Wow. What the hell was that, huh?" he said.

I said, "I'll say."

My phone rang. I about jumped out of my skin, thinking for a second that it might be Ree. It was Zach, though, telling me to call Regina and have her go to the hospital. "Do you have Regina's phone number?" he said.

"Uh, hold on. Let me get Olivia's phone." I dug it out of her purse and looked up Regina's number. "Got it," I said. "How is Olivia doing?"

"We're still in the ambulance. I think she's going to be okay. I'll keep you posted."

"Alright, thanks. 'Bye." I hung up and called Regina.

She answered on the first ring. "Olivia? Where have you been? Mother is frantic. Are you okay? Where are you?"

"Hi, Regina. It's Star. Listen, I really hate to call with bad news, but---"

"Oh, my god. What's wrong? Where's Olivia? What has she done?"

"Uh, she's on her way to the hospital. Can you go there? Christus St. Vincent. Yeah, the emergency room."

"Okay. What's wrong?"

I didn't know how you were supposed to say this kind of thing, so I just said it straight out. "She overdosed on Tylenol."

It was hard to hear commanding, in-charge Regina's voice break. She said, "Oh, my god. She went off her meds again, didn't she?"

Peter said, "Tell her... Wait. Can I talk to her?"

I was more than happy to hand him Olivia's phone. He said, "Hi, Regina. This is Peter Thomas. You might remember me? Anyway, just wanted to let you know that Olivia was here when she, well we *think* she took a bunch of Tylenol. She was breathing and even talking to us a little bit when the paramedics got here. Yeah. Just wanted to let you know. Okay, Regina. 'Bye."

Then Peter turned to me. "I think we need a drink."

"I think we definitely do."

We went back to the living room and Peter poured us each an overly full glass of wine. "I hope you like Merlot. It's the only booze we've got in the house right now."

"Thanks," I said. I didn't know what kind of wine I liked. "Do you want to watch something else?" *Cops* was just too much right now. We'd had enough of emergency services for one night.

"Definitely," he said.

I took a couple of sips, wanting the wine buzz to calm me down right away. But it was too strong to drink very fast. That Regina. She could be bossy but that was a damn sister who cared.

I said, "Do you know what Regina meant, about Olivia's meds?"

"Oh, psych meds, no doubt. Olivia had to be hospitalized for a while in high school, you know. When Zach broke up with her. Zach still blames himself. He says he was young and stupid and didn't break up with her very nicely. I think that's why he jumped when she called. Trying to make it up to her or something."

"Oh." It was too complicated a subject for me right then. I took a couple more sips of wine. It seemed pretty clear, though, that Olivia wouldn't be released for a while. And that I didn't belong here without her.

Peter was flipping through channels. He stopped on an old *Seinfeld* episode, the one where Elaine does the hilariously awkward moves out on the dance floor. "Want to watch this?" he said.

I said, "That looks perfect to me."

#

Olivia stole my money. I couldn't fucking believe it. I had a secret emergency stash, a couple hundred bucks left from my cleaning and dog sitting pay from Celia. I kept it in my purse, in a little zipper pouch I'd made with Bonnie Sue. Looking back, I guess that was a too obvious place to keep it. But I didn't think Olivia would rip me off.

She knew damn well I'd help her out if she really needed it anyway. She should have known that. In fact, I think spending some of my stash on food for both of us after we got kicked out of Melinda's was how Olivia learned that I had money in the first place.

I'd been packing up my stuff and Olivia's stuff at Zach and Peter's place. I stopped to count my money, since how much I still had left might make a difference in whatever next move I'd take. Well, my little zipper money pouch was missing from my purse. I finally found it in the trunk of Olivia's car, when I remembered we had some dirty clothes in there. I thought I'd wash them before I left, since Zach and Peter had a washer and dryer in their apartment. My money pouch was buttoned up in the pocket of a pair of Olivia's shorts.

I tried to think of a scenario where it could be some kind of misunderstanding, where Olivia had not really taken my last damn dollar. I couldn't, though. It wasn't a misunderstanding.

When Regina called to say she was coming to get Olivia's things, I left them outside Zach and Peter's door. Then I blocked both Olivia and Regina on my phone. Now I had nobody here.

It was time to go home.

#

Bonnie Sue didn't call me back right away but I figured she was probably at work and not allowed to take calls. Or maybe she was driving, or had her head under the hairdryer at the hairdresser's. But I was surprised when 24 hours went by with no return phone call. I called again and left another message.

That time, my phone did ring right away and it was Bonnie Sue. I felt a rush of joy at hearing her voice. I expected a lot of emotion, and for her to demand to know where I was and who I was with. Then she'd zoom right over and rescue me.

She said, "Star. How have you been, hon?"

"Bonnie Sue! Oh, my god. I've missed you so much. And I've missed Big Mom-Mom and my dad, too. All of you! Ree's gone and I really want to come home. Can you come and get me? I'm in Santa Fe." It was a three-hour drive but I could find something to do for three hours.

I thought I heard a little… laugh? No, most likely, she just cleared her throat. She said "Well, I'm in Kentucky, so I don't think I can do that."

"Oh. Um, I guess I could come to Kentucky." I didn't expect to go to Kentucky. I expected her to say oh no, don't be silly, sugar britches. I'll just cut my trip short. After all, I can go to Kentucky any old time. Then she'd probably add on something about how it would be her pleasure.

There was a long pause. Then, she said, "I appreciate the thought, hon, but I don't think that's the best idea. See, we don't really have the extra room here right now." Her voice sounded tired, not excited. Was she sick?

My stomach started getting that slinky feeling. I was waiting for her to tell me the plan, who she'd send to come get me right away instead of herself, then. Maybe she'd send my dad, for example. Or even Big Mom-Mom. She didn't say anything else, though. Something was very wrong. I said, "Oh. Well, when are you going back home?"

"I am back home. You see, your dad and I are divorced. And we're both re-married, to other people now."

"What? Are you kidding? When did all this happen?"

"Well, Star, it's been a while. You left that last time, what's it been, four years ago now?"

"Yeah. I guess it has been four years." I heard a little kid in the background, asking Meemaw for a cookie.

"Listen hon, I can't talk right now. I've got my husband's daughter and her husband here with their little ones. We're just about to sit down to supper."

Still in shock, I said, "Oh. Okay. I guess I'll… I guess I'll let you go, then."

She said, "'Bye, hon. You take care now, hear? And send my regards to Big Mom-Mom." She didn't offer to call me back later.

The phone went dead. I sat there for a while, in a daze. I always thought Bonnie Sue would be there in the background, waiting around for me if I ever needed her. It had never crossed my mind that she might not be.

#

The second person who picked me up on my journey from Santa Fe to Roswell called herself Aunt Edie. She said, "All right, young lady. Aunt Edie's gonna sit right here and watch until you're safely in the house."

"Oh, I'll be fine. Even if nobody's home, I've got loads of other family around here. Thanks again for the ride." I grabbed my stuff and shut the car door, though she'd started talking again. I rushed away in the opposite direction of my dad's house. I wanted to be sure to throw her off my trail for good.

I'd been relieved when she picked me up, an older woman who offered to take me right to my dad's door. You just couldn't trust strange men. But then I'd had to put up with two hours of her lecturing. She scolded me for hitchhiking. Then she interrogated me about my background, in embarrassing detail. Finally, she moved on to drill me about where I thought my life was headed now. I got the idea that picking up a ragamuffin like me and trying to straighten me out was highly exciting for the old girl. She was in no hurry to give it up.

I scurried down one street, then turned onto another. My bags were getting heavy, so I stopped in at the corner convenience store, which I remembered as having a little dining area. I bought a Coke and sat there for a good twenty minutes, before heading back in the direction I'd come. If Aunt Edie got a chance, I could see her following me to my dad's door to snitch on me for hitchhiking.

After the shocking and painful brush-off from Bonnie Sue, I stopped assuming that my dad would want to take me in either, especially if he could easily get out of it. I decided it was a better bet to just show up at his door.

I wanted a real home, and I wanted it to be the same home for more than a couple of days or months at a time, dammit. The best thing I could even imagine was living in the same house and the same town with the same people around for years and years. Better yet, forever.

My dad's front door had been painted bright red and there was new landscaping across the front of the house, a bed of gravelly rocks and cactus-like shrubs, with a wood border. I snickered at the thought of what Ree would think about it.

That look she'd get on her face, like she was stunned speechless at such examples of pointless idiocy. To her, changing the door color and putting in ornamental plants was about the same as spray painting the grass.

Then I felt the familiar pang that I always got when I remembered Ree, who seemed to have ditched me for good this time. She would most likely never see the funny new domestic livestock creations in front of my dad's house.

And then, what if my dad wasn't the one who'd made the changes to the front of the house? What if he'd moved away, just like Bonnie Sue did? I set my bags down, took a deep breath and rang the doorbell.

A woman opened the door a crack, leaving the chain lock in place. Or I should say, a nose answered the door, since that was about all I could see, A long, pointy beak. She said, "Yes?" She sounded irritated.

"Hello. Um, I'm Star. Frank Garza's daughter?"

She slammed the door in my face!

The bee buzzing started up in my mind. Who the fuck did she think she was? This was my dad's house and I was his minor child. I had way more right to be here than she did. That is, if she was my dad's new wife. How dare the old hag make me stand outside and figure out how to navigate her nastiness. I vowed to get rid of her. I'd run her off as soon as possible.

It seemed like a long time before my dad came to the door but maybe it wasn't. I was too upset to know how long it took him.

His face lit up. He said, "Mijita! Estrellita! My leetle Star!" He pulled me in, pulled my bags in, then pulled me into a big bear hug. The look of joy on his face seemed real. I felt great then, for the first time in a while. For a minute, anyway.

The cruel dad-poacher sat in Bonnie Sue's usual place on the sofa. She was glueing pointy, blood-colored artificial nails onto her real fingernails. Claws. Talons. And that beak. Clearly, the bitch was a bird of prey. A harpy? A vulture? I'd have to look up if those fit the description.

"Thees is my wife, Thelma," my dad said, like it was some kind of wonderful news.

And *Thelma?* Really? Was it 1942? My dad's face looked so open and happy, though. For him, I forced myself to say, "Hello, Thelma. Nice to meet you."

"Hello," she snipped, like she was constipated or something. She probably needed Aunt Edie to trap her in the car and talk to her about her life choices.

"I call Mama!" my dad said, the tension in the room going right over his head. Or maybe he just acted like it did. Bonnie Sue used to get so mad at him, when he'd try to duck out of confrontations.

He went in his bedroom and shut the door. When he came back a few minutes later, he was on the phone with Big Mom-Mom. He said she wanted to talk to me, and handed me his phone.

Big Mom-Mom sing-songed in my ear, "Star! Oh, my stars. If it isn't the star of the show!"

That made me smile. She said, "Listen, sweet pea, old Big Mom-Mom's not feeling so good right now. How about you come over and spend the night here with me. I could really use the help, huh? And the company, of course. Ooh, and I have chocolate chip cookies."

I said sure, that I'd be right there. What else could I do, tell the grandmother I hadn't seen in four years that no, actually, I wouldn't go over there and help her? Besides, I didn't feel welcome at my dad's place. Not by the creature who had replaced Bonnie Sue, at least. But at the same time, I was a bit disappointed. I'd planned to stick around and think up sly ways to torment the hag.

#

I didn't go back to my dad's house. Apparently, Thelma wanted him all to herself. She didn't want me around. She didn't want Big Mom-Mom around, either. My dad stopped by to see us a couple of times a week. He'd help with things, like picking up groceries or Big Mom-Mom's medicine when she didn't feel well enough to go out. But he never stayed long. I didn't know if Thelma knew about it but my guess was that she did not.

Big Mom-Mom had a heart condition now but she still insisted on doing most of the cooking and housework anyway. Which I understood. Just like me, she liked her routines. She just did things slower than she used to and took more breaks. She'd probably only said she needed my help that first day to spare my feelings about no longer being welcome in my dad's home.

I wished I could spare Big Mom-Mom's feelings, too. It was sad to see her being restricted to her own side of the property line. She used to seem so happy being part of the family, with her and Bonnie Sue in and out of each other's houses for meals or chit-chat and whatever. She was quieter now. Big Mom-Mom was such a kind, big-hearted person. I couldn't believe anyone would not want her around. Bonnie Sue had been gone for three years but Big Mom-Mom talked about her like she'd just seen her the other day.

#

A couple of weeks later, it was like I was in a whole different world again. I got on the school bus and followed my survival plan. My plan was, first of all, to sit as close to the front of the bus as possible. I'd sit at the front of the room in my classes, too. People messed with you less anywhere, when you were near the person in charge.

Then, I'd work on the lessons that I'd printed out from my new online GED course. I'd work on my lessons on the bus, in between classes and at lunch. I'd keep my focus on my goal and try to blend in with the scenery at school, just try to be invisible. That was how I'd make it through the next six months.

I already had a plan, until my dad and Big Mom-Mom interfered. It was to sign up for an online GED course, which I did. And my dad seemed happy to pay for it, I'll give him that. However, you had to be sixteen to actually take the GED exam and receive your high school equivalency. That was what the trouble was over. I wouldn't be sixteen until mid-February, which was nearly six months away.

So, I'd planned to just take the online GED course, then take the GED exam itself as soon as I turned sixteen. I wanted to get on with it. I'd get my GED and then I could go to school for interior design. In the meantime, maybe I could get a job and make some money, when I wasn't studying. Baby-sitting or cleaning houses, at least. I thought it was a great plan and I was jazzed about it.

I wasn't like other kids. Most of them had been in school for many years. They'd never lived free or been itinerant or lived with their boyfriend. I didn't know what the right thing was to say, or do, or wear at school. I didn't fit in with those kids and I was afraid of them. They could be mean.

But my dad, who didn't even care enough about me to have me in his home, stuck his big nose into it and stubbornly refused to let me follow my plan. No doubt it was only because Big Mom-Mom told him what to say, which pissed me off even more. I'd learned she had a sterner side, hidden behind her jolly grandma self. I guess I just never saw it before because Bonnie Sue had always been the one in charge of me. But now I had to go to high school until I turned sixteen and was able to take the GED exam.

There was absolutely no way around it, according to my dad and Big Mom-Mom. What really pissed me off was that they wouldn't even give me a logical reason. It was *just because.*

I wasn't in a position where I could argue very much, either. When it came down to it, I really didn't know either of them that well. My main person after Ree had always been Bonnie Sue. So here I was, showing up out of nowhere, nearly grown, disrupting my dad and Big Mom-Mom's lives. My dad already made it clear that he picked his new wife over me. Apparently, I didn't have a chance at getting rid of her but she was able to easily get rid of me. So what would stop my dad and Big Mom-Mom from just deciding, *Nah, you're too much, after all. You just have to go.* You couldn't argue too much with an old lady who had a heart condition, anyway.

It seriously crossed my mind that this whole family reunion was just not meant to be. I thought about just taking off and going on some time free. That's how mad I was about them making me go back to school. Damn, I'd rather go to juvie than to high school. I'd probably fit in better there. After all, I knew how to make pruno.

But in the end, I decided to stay. My dad and Big Mom-Mom were putting me through a rough time that I didn't need. But I knew it was only because they just didn't understand. And even with their school attendance requirement, I still liked living in a stable, safe, comfortable house a lot more than I liked the bird of passage lifestyle, where you had a rough time, all the time. I didn't want to go on time free by myself.

So, here I was, on the school bus for my first day of the tenth grade, three weeks after the school year started.

After the bus dropped us off at school, I learned that we were supposed to go to the cafeteria in the morning and stay there until the bell rang. You could get something to eat or drink in the morning, if you wanted, but I didn't know that and didn't bring any money. I hated these unstructured times. I'd have to figure out what table to sit at, for one thing, when I might be taking somebody's usual place. And I couldn't just stick my nose in my GED study stuff when I was standing up in the busy cafeteria. My mind bees buzzed over the big room full of tables, and all the people, and the noise. I felt my sock for my pocketknife, out of habit, but caught myself before pulling it out. I decided to go stand around in the bathroom instead.

I kind of slumped in the corner of the girls' restroom, trying to focus on a GED Math lesson at the same time I tried not to look like a weirdo who hung out in the restroom.

"Star? Is that you? someone said.

"Brynn?"

"Oh, gee. I thought that was you!" she said. She had pink plastic butterfly barrettes in her hair, like you'd expect on a ten-year-old. I suddenly felt quite with-it, compared to Brynn.

"What's funny?" she said, looking confused.

"What? Oh, nothing. I'm just happy to see you." I felt bad for my catty thoughts then, about the only person who'd wanted to talk to me here so far.

#

Brynn and I rode the same bus. I probably just didn't see her that first morning because I'd deliberately kept my attention on my GED lessons.

But she got off at my stop with me that first afternoon. Brynn still seemed young for her age, even four years later. She was still super nice anyway, though. And here she was, helping me get used to a new school, all over again.

I had her wait outside while I went in and asked if she could come in. I didn't know if I could bring friends home.

Big Mom-Mom seemed delighted. She said, "Oh, Miss Annette's girl! Of course she can come in, sweet pea. Any time."

On a whim, Big Mom-Mom offered to take us to get our nails done. She made Brynn call to get her mom's permission first. Then Brynn's mom, Miss Annette, ended up coming along, too. It was Brynn's first time and she was thrilled with her shiny, pale pink gel nails. I got a gold shade, Miss Annette got red and Big Mom-Mom got bright, glittery purple. She was joking around and jolly, like her old self again.

Then she treated us all to pizza on the way home. It reminded me of the happy times we used to have when Bonnie Sue was around. I hoped we could bring more of that back, even if it was with different people.

I was surprised to be feeling so much better about school, especially after only one day of it. Later that night, after Brynn and Miss Annette left, Big Mom-Mom said, "There, see. High school's not so bad, is it?"

I didn't want to say she was right because I'd still much rather do things my way. And, of course, we could have just invited Brynn and Miss Annette over anyway. Having Brynn around at school made me a lot less anxious about it, though. It was easier to get through the school day when I knew I'd have her with me for at least part of the day. I just kinda smiled, without saying either yes or no.

Big Mom-Mom said, "Well. If I'm wrong in the end, I'll owe you an apology. I just feel like you've missed out enough already, hon. Since you're our responsibility now, I wanted to be sure you got at least that little piece of what all the other kids got. I want you on the inside of it all, not on the outside, looking in. And you don't have to rush on to adulthood, either. If you change your mind, you can take those other two and a half years of high school, too."

She seemed tired out, after saying all that. She asked me to bring the pillow and blanket from her bed, so she could lie on the sofa and watch TV for a while.

I still liked my idea better. But I guess she did have a point. I don't know why she didn't tell me all that in the first place.

#

It was chilly on Big Mom-Mom's patio, which I guess was to be expected in November. I sipped my chai with milk, and warmed my hands on the mug's heat while I waited for Thelma. Ah, there she was. I saw her curtain move. No doubt she was looking for me.

A minute later, she stepped out onto her patio, wrapped in a shawl. She stood facing me, hands on hips. Then she gave me the finger.

I nodded in polite acknowledgement. I had a special variation for her today. I stood up, then turn away from her, bent over, and reach backwards between my legs to flip her off in return.

She nodded. Then we both went back into our houses.

This started a few weeks ago, when I happened to be doing my GED work at Big Mom-Mom's patio table. Thelma was out in her and my dad's back yard for some reason and, I don't know, her bird face annoyed me, so I flipped her off. I could see that it made her laugh, which surprised me. It surprised me even more when she flipped me off back.

Now it's a thing. Not every day but most days. I look out the window after school to see if she's out there, waiting for me. I know she watches for me, too. Fuck you, Thelma. And have a nice evening.

#

Brynn and I were in the cafeteria one morning before school, when Selena came by and plopped herself down at our table.

She said, "Remember me?"

"Yeah! How've you been, girl?" I said, adding the "girl" part to try to sound with-it. I almost said "bitch," since she and Madison used to call each other that in elementary school and it seemed super cool at the time. It probably wouldn't come across very well now, though.

She said, "Eh. Not much. Same day, different shit. You know. Wait… Well, you know what I mean." I was surprised she sat with us or even remembered me. She probably had plenty of popular people to sit with. I remembered how she'd turned down my offers of friendship before. But I guess it would be dumb to hang on to kid stuff like that.

She said, "So, there's a party Friday night and it's gonna be huge. Ten bucks at the door. I'll draw you a map if you want to come."

"Oh, wow. I don't know. Do you need an answer right now?"

She kind of laughed. "I don't need an answer at all You just come if you come. Hmm. You looked like a partier to me, like you'd already know how the parties go."

"I guess I am. Sort of. Okay, why don't you give me directions, then."

She started writing the directions on a napkin, describing them as she wrote.

I knew the streets and how to get there, but of course I didn't know the address of that particular house.

She said, "It starts when the sun goes down. Oh, and dress warm. It's mostly outside."

I said, "Okay. Thanks."

But she was already on to the next table. I said to Brynn, "Want to go?"

Brynn had stuck her nose in a book and didn't seem to hear me. I asked her again.

She said, "I don't think so. It's not really my kind of thing."

Come to think of it, Selena didn't say anything to Brynn. She'd only talked to me.

Brynn hardly spoke to me for the rest of the day. I think she was mad. But the next morning, she seemed almost back to her usual self. It didn't take much to figure out that Brynn didn't fit in with Selena and the rest of the stoners. Maybe it hurt Brynn's feelings to think I was branching out without her.

I couldn't wait to go to the party, though. It was only a few blocks from Big Mom-Mom's house so I could walk over there.

#

On the bus home from school on Friday, I still wasn't sure how I'd get around Big Mom-Mom. I could definitely see her insisting on driving me to the party herself or insisting on speaking to the parents. The best I could do would probably be to sneak out after Big Mom-Mom went to bed, which was usually around ten o'clock. At least I'd get to go to the party for a while.

But when I got home from school, Big Mom-Mom's car was gone and the door was locked.

I had to use the key under the potted plant on the front porch to get in. Big Mom-Mom left me a note on the kitchen counter. She was at a doctor's appointment.

I couldn't believe my great good luck. If she didn't get home before I made it out of here, that is. I rushed to my room and changed into a sexy outfit from my Devon days. Then I remembered Selena said the party was mostly outside, and I changed into some warm, heavy, unsexy clothes instead, cursing the whole time and hoping Big Mom-Mom didn't come home. I grabbed Ree's Native poncho too, the one she'd left behind at the campsite.

It smelled like Ree, or that woodsy smell that reminded me of her, anyway. The Taos scent: wood smoke, pine and a touch of cinnamon or something like it. I didn't have time to dwell on it, though.

I went to the kitchen and wrote in the space left on Big Mom-Mom's note to me:

I just lucked into a babysitting gig! Probably won't be home until late. Love you!

I hurried out of the house and jogged a few blocks before slowing down. I was headed for the library, for somewhere to hang out until it got dark out. If Big Mom-Mom asked about the babysitting job, I decided to say some girl at school needed somebody to fill in for her. The thing was, I didn't really know what was or wasn't allowed at Big Mom-Mom's house. I hadn't tried that many things out yet because I didn't want to rock the boat. But her insisting that I go to school, even though I had a solid alternative plan, made me think I shouldn't expect much more freedom that Bonnie Sue used to give me, which wasn't much at all.

At the library, I logged into a computer and worked on my GED lessons. I'd still most likely stick with my plan to get done with high school and on to studying interior design as soon as possible. But who knew for sure. I didn't turn sixteen for three more months so I'd see how I felt then. I was still sure enough about the GED to keep studying for it though, even though it was boring as hell. I was about halfway through the course now, on all four subjects.

It got dark super early now in mid-November, like, by five p.m. In my rush to escape from the house, I didn't even think about dinner. But I had a few bucks on me, so after studying for a while, I decided to grab something at the convenience store.

I wasn't crazy about roaming around outside, especially after dark and when it was cold out. I just couldn't wait to drive. I'd have to start studying for that test, too. I microwaved a burrito and got a Coke at the convenience store but all three booths there were taken, so I had to eat standing up. Then it was dark out and I made my way to the party.

"Hey, Star! Estrella! Que pasa, chica?" Selena yelled, as soon as I'd paid my ten bucks and got my hand stamped. She ran over and hugged me, seeming thrilled to see me. She seemed wasted already and it wasn't even six p.m.

"Hey, Selena. Oh, whoa," I said, as her over-the-top greeting nearly knocked me down. I looked around for an excuse to get away from her.

There were a couple dozen people so far. There was also a band, a bonfire and a keg. It was a big yard but it was still in a subdivision, not far away from neighbors, not somewhere you were likely to get away with a bunch of minors being loud and drunk for long, I thought. I decided to enjoy it while it lasted though, after scoping out a couple of good escape routes for if the cops showed up.

I saw the line for the keg and told Selena I'd be right back, which was a lie. While I was standing in line, some guy offered to get me a cup. He was tall and blonde-ish. I said okay because it would seem snotty not to. But I was put off by him at first. He was handsome enough but he looked too much like Devon.

He got me a big disposable plastic cup. They were stacked up by the keg, where you'd use them anyway, so I guess it was just his way of trying to get my attention. "Thanks," I said. It was too loud now to try to say very much. The band had started screaming instead of playing and singing.

They stood in a circle, facing each other and flat-out screamed, on and on, all four of them. People were standing around them, nodding along like they'd do to music.

"What's your name?" The Devon-ish said, three times before I could hear him, though he was standing close enough to kiss me.

"Star. What's yours?"

"Devon."

"What? No. Not Devon. Please, anything but Devon."

He said, "Huh?"

We were near the front of the keg line now. He held his finger up like "Hold that thought." He filled my cup with beer and handed it back to me, then filled his own cup. He met my gaze, then pointed at the house next door.

I didn't really understand what was going on but he took my hand and I followed along, I guess just because I didn't have any better ideas. I didn't like it out here. It was cold and the screaming band was fucking obnoxious.

He led me next door, through the unfenced backyard, and then to a travel trailer that sat on its own slab, at a distance from the house.

I didn't know about this at all. He was cute and I felt like he had a gentle way about him. But that didn't mean anything, really. It still seemed the kind of situation that could get you on *Forensics Files.*

"Um, I have to go," I said, hurrying towards the driveway and the street beyond.

"Ah. Too secluded?"

I kept walking, fast, like I didn't hear him.

He called after me, "Wait! Let's walk to the convenience store, then. Let me buy you a Coke."

At least we'd be out in public then, walking down streets that were full of houses. I grabbed my pocketknife out of my sock, opened it and stuck it in my front pocket, where I could keep a grip on it under the poncho. I said, "Okay."

We'd only gone a few houses down when two cop cars rode by and pulled up in front of the party house. After they passed, he said, "Drink up. Cheers!" We guzzled our beers, then dropped the cups.

It turned out his name was Kevin, not Devon. I said, "Oh good. I can keep talking to you, then."

"Devon is an ex, I take it?"

"Yep."

"Hmm. Sounds like there's a story there."

"Yep."

"So, do you go to Roswell High?"

"Yep."

He laughed at my string of "Yeps," but saying any more of them in a row would probably be rude so I asked him if he went to Roswell High, too.

"Yeah, but not for much longer. I'll graduate early, so this is my last semester."

"Wow, really? Mine, too. Well, in a different way, though."

We sat in a booth at the convenience store for a few hours, drinking sodas and talking and then he walked me home. I had him leave me at the corner, in case Big Mom-Mom was watching for me.

After giving him my phone number, I practically floated the rest of the way home. Meeting somebody new and wonderful was such a high. But it also came with worries about…everything.

What did he mean by this thing he said or that thing he did. Would he really call? How interested was he in me?

Big Mom-Mom had left the porch light on for me. I was glad she'd gone to bed instead of waiting up. My note was still on the counter and Big Mom-Mom had drawn a heart on it.

It took me a long time to get all the ink off my hand, where it was stamped to show I'd paid to get into the keg party. I didn't want to have to try and explain it to Big Mom-Mom. I finally got the last traces of it off with nail polish remover.

#

Kevin called me the next day, which was a Saturday, and again on Sunday. He had to work both nights. He worked at the mozzarella plant, the same place as my dad. He even knew my dad. That could come in handy. Maybe he could gather intel that would help me run Thelma off.

You never knew. The only other Thelmas I'd ever heard of were the one on the old Scooby Doo cartoons and the one in the movie, *Thelma & Louise*. At the end of the movie, Thelma and Louise drove off a cliff.

I told Big Mom-Mom I'd met a guy at school and she seemed really pleased. She said, "You should get on birth control," which shocked me.

But who wanted to talk about birth control with their grandmother. I put my fingers in my ears and said, "Wah-wah-wah" until she laughed and moved on to a different topic.

The next week, she suggested I invite Kevin to Thanksgiving dinner but I didn't. I wanted to keep him to myself, at least for a while. Big Mom-Mom was mostly lovely but she also seemed lonesome. I really liked having her join in when it was just me and Brynn but picturing her sitting there in between me and Kevin did not appeal to me. I had other things in mind to do with Kevin, like have lots of nasty sex with him in his camper home, in his parents' back yard.

Since it would be just the two of us, Big Mom-Mom decided we should go to a restaurant buffet for Thanksgiving. It seemed less sad than cooking half the day, then sitting there thinking about how the other half of our family refused to even share a holiday meal with us. It would suck not to have any leftovers for later, though.

#

I started riding to and from school with Kevin and we sat together in the cafeteria in the mornings, too. Brynn sat with us a couple of times and then she just didn't anymore. I was too caught up with Kevin to think much about it.

Selena stopped by our table one morning to take credit for setting the two of us up, although she hadn't. She said, "Oh my god, I feel like your auntie!" And "I feel like the mother of the bride. And the groom!"

Mainly just to change the topic, I said, "Hey, whatever happened to that Madison girl? The two of you used to be like twins, practically."

"Oh, Madison. Wow. I haven't thought about her in forever. She moved away."

I said, "Aww," though I hadn't liked Madison, at least not after I caught on that she didn't like me. I wondered what she'd be like now, though. Selena had definitely gone downhill. It seemed like the fifth grade had been the high point of her life or something. Kevin and I already had a good laugh about how impossibly cool and sophisticated I used to think Selena was.

She said, "Well, gotta go, kids. Name your firstborn after me!"

As she walked away, I made a face at Kevin.

Brynn came over then and filled Selena's vacated seat, like Kevin and I were having visiting hours today only or something. Another girl sat down beside her. Brynn said, "Hi. Hey, do you remember Maria José here, from elementary school?"

"Well, I knew a Maria José but I don't think it was this Maria José. Anyway, hi, to both of you. What's up?"

Brynn said, "Oh, not much. Maria José thinks it was your mom who was dancing up on the bluff that day. You know, when the whole school dropped everything to watch her. Was it your mom? It was such a beautiful dance."

"Huh? Heck no, that wouldn't have been my mother. I don't remember anyone dancing on a bluff, anyway. Hey, that's a pretty necklace, Brynn. Is it new?" It was a string of pink, heart-shaped beads. I was anxious to change the subject from Ree dancing on the bluff. It was embarrassing, even without the naked part.

Maria José said, "I got a nose job. That's probably why you don't recognize me. Technically, it's called a rhinoplasty. I couldn't breathe right.'

I said, "Oh, yeah. I think I recognize you now." I recognized her in the first place. I just didn't want to admit it because I didn't like her. Parrot beak or not, she was as annoying as ever.

If anyone was going to bring up one of the most embarrassing events of my life, naturally it would be Maria José, the first chance she got. She was just that kind of girl.

Brynn said, "I made this. You weren't home so my mom took me and Maria José to the bead shop without you." She sounded a little sulky. It took me a sec to realize she was taking about her necklace.

"Aw, shucks. Guess I missed out big time." I felt Kevin sort of jiggle beside me, laughing. He recognized my sneaky sarcasm but Brynn wouldn't.

I gave him an elbow jab, also sneakily. I was starting to feel lousy about taking a dig at Brynn that I knew she wouldn't even understand. She was a very trustworthy, nice girl and didn't deserve to be mocked.

But I just felt like I was with my kid sister around her. I could only relate to her in a limited way. Maria José was probably a better friend for her. Of course, I couldn't tell Brynn that. I resented that, the times when it seemed like it wouldn't be acceptable to just say the truth to people. It seemed like there were a lot of times like that.

#

"Oh, really?" I said, perking up. We were in Kevin's camper, trying to settle down to our studies after doing it twice. After a session of doing it was completed, Kevin usually wanted to drift off to sleep for a while and I always wanted fast food, though it varied between Taco Bell, Kentucky Fried Chicken and McDonald's. I usually won. But it was getting late and finals week was coming up. Not that either of us was in any danger of flunking out or anything. We were just both kind of perfectionists, in that way. We both liked to do things right.

We'd barely settled in with our school work when Kevin's little brother, Calvin, starting trying to rock the camper again, pushing on it from outside. Kevin had to go chase him off.

Calvin was twelve, at that age where he was starting to get obsessed with sex, and his way of handling it was constantly annoying us. That's what Kevin thought, anyway. I thought the boy probably needed to be turned into a dog for a while, so he'd learn that he was in a pack, and also the least important member of the pack at this time. I'd told Kevin that whole story, with Ree and Harley.

Kevin seemed equally horrified and delighted, which to me, was the correct response. Especially compared to Devon's boring outrage and attempts to involve himself in my relationship with my mother. I sort of blamed Devon for Ree leaving my life completely. Then again, maybe Kevin would act differently too, if there had been any mother-daughter relationship left for him to involve himself in.

Either way, I felt like Kevin was a definite improvement over Devon. Kevin seemed smarter, in a way that made him more interested in other points of view on various topics, rather than always thinking there was nothing more to any topic besides the opinions he already held. Also, Kevin and I both intended to go for higher education and have professional careers.

Anyway, I quit thinking about all that when Kevin told me that my dad and Thelma planned to spend Christmas in the Florida Keys. My dad didn't know Kevin and I were dating. Of course, that was as it should be. Kevin was to collect intel on my dad, not give him intel on me.

I said, "Oh, really? When are they leaving?" This was exciting news.

"Um, I'm not sure." I thought Kevin looked a little scared, which was kind of hot, in a not-hot way. Which made sense to me at the time.

I wanted my bedroom furniture set, which as far as I knew, was still in my dad's house. It was a solid piece of…solidness in my life. It was something of mine that had been around for years, when I had very few things like that. I knew better than to just come out and ask for it, though. That would be stupid because Thelma ran things over there and she was a bitch.

Therefore, she should always be expected to act like a bitch, whenever given a choice. I didn't intend to give her a choice.

I said, "What days is my dad off work? I'm gonna get my furniture."

He kind of whistled. He said, "You go to jail for shit like that."

"Hmm. Good point. I know, I'll make Big Mom-Mom get it. She even still has a key to my dad's house. It's in the kitchen junk drawer. Even my pussy-wussy birth father wouldn't let Thelma have his dear old mother tossed in the slammer."

"Star…" He shook his head.

I said, "You just find out his vacation days. You better. Or else no more you-know-what for you."

He sighed deeply, then turned back to his studying.

I was too excited to focus on mine.

#

"Damn it, Selena. Pay attention to the walls."

"I'm trying. Sor-ree!"

I knew I shouldn't have let her get high first. Then again, if she hadn't been high, she might not have said yes. It was impossible to know for sure.

Finally, we got my twin bed frame, headboard, mattress and bedding into Big Mom-Mom's garage. We managed to make all three of the trips it took without me killing or seriously maiming Selena. But my god, that girl could whine. It was cold out, the mattress was too heavy, she needed a rest.

We still had to get the dresser and the nightstand. I decided to leave the desk and chair. They were child-sized and would look silly in my bedroom at Big Mom-Mom's.

I nearly cried when I saw it, my red bedroom that Bonnie Sue and I had put so much happy effort into putting together. I was surprised that everything was still there. I thought for sure old buzzard face Thelma would have cleared out all traces of my dad's family during her hostile takeover.

"I'm thirsty," Selena said. "I have to go tinkle."

We were going back into my dad's house again, through his back door. I said, "Oh, all right. Hurry up, though. We need to get this shit done before Big Mom-Mom catches us."

"What? How the fuck do you plan to keep her from catching you? I mean, it's *furniture*. It's large. It's in her garage. She is going to catch you." Selena fell into a laughing fit over what she though was my glaring dumbness.

"Well, duh. I just don't want her to catch us in the act of moving the furniture between houses. Because then she'll ask questions and then I'll either have to lie to her, or else she'll make us put it all back. Remember, it's her key. And obviously, she didn't give me permission to use it."

Selena said, "Ugh. Stop confusing me."

"It's only confusing when you look at it in one big clump. The thing is, you have to break things down, see? First, we just get the damn furniture. Possession is nine tenths of the law, you know."

She made a face at me, then went into the bathroom. I took a minute to look around. The one time I'd been in my dad's house since I'd been back in Roswell was only for a few minutes. And there had been too much going on then for me to notice the decor.

The living room and dining room furniture were the same but the stuff on the walls and the knick-knacks were gone. I guessed Bonnie Sue took the small stuff back to Kentucky with her but left the big items. And Thelma, having no soul, wasn't into home décor, naturally. Thelma didn't seem to me like the type who would want to make a house into a home. She seemed more into conquering and destroying things like home, family and beauty. Anything good, basically.

I found a bottle of tequila in the pantry, and some 7-Up in the fridge. I fixed a strong drink. I needed to get this job finished.

When Selena came out, I said, "All right, I'll put you out of your misery. I'll take the drawers out of the dresser. Then you can just help me carry the dresser itself. This delightful alcoholic beverage will be waiting for you back here, as your well-earned reward, girly. Then I can carry the drawers myself."

Selena didn't follow instructions. She grabbed the drink out of my hand and slurped down half of it. Then she surprised me and said, "Nah. Let's do it together." She helped me finish it up, in three more trips.

We said our good-byes at the garage and I tip-toed into the kitchen. I slipped my dad's house key back into the junk drawer.

Soon after that, I sat down to dinner with Big Mom-Mom. I didn't know what I was happier about, getting my furniture back or giving a well-deserved slap to fucking Thelma. Big Mom-Mom said, "You sure seem chipper this evening."

I blurted, "My bedroom furniture's in the garage. From my dad's house." *Ugh. Stupid-ass.*

Big Mom-Mom said, "Oh, how nice. But why didn't your dad come in and say hello?"

"Oh! Excuse me a second." I jumped out of my chair, snatched up my phone and rushed to my bedroom, like I had some urgent phone business to tend to. That way, I avoided having to lie to Big Mom-Mom. It hit me then, that this was the kind of tactic my dad was so good at.

I returned to the table babbling about Christmas, which was coming up in only ten more days. Hopefully, that would be a more interesting topic to Big Mom-Mom than my old bedroom furniture.

#

We were on the drive home from school, Kevin and I. I was relieved when he seemed to find the bedroom furniture heist funny, now that it was in the past and I hadn't dragged him into it. I was in a great mood because we were now officially on Christmas break. Even better, Kevin was through with high school completely. I hoped to be done with it too, in just a couple more months.

I hated to think about him going away to college but I figured these were necessary growing pains. Maybe I could even join him there soon. We hadn't gotten around to making our plans yet but very, very soon, we'd both be done with this kiddie bullshit and on to our real life together.

I turned the tunes up in his truck and sang along with Mariah Carey's "All I Want for Christmas is You," squeezing Kevin's leg or, um, other parts of Kevin, in time with the music. I was wondering what Kevin got me for Christmas. It was only three days away now.

I secretly wished for a promise ring. We hadn't been together long enough for an engagement ring, or any ring, really, under normal circumstances. But these were special circumstances, since he was going away. I'd gotten him a bottle of aftershave, a big tin full of different kinds of nuts and a new wallet, since his was falling apart. Nothing too exciting but it was all I could think of that was in my budget. His gifts were wrapped and ready to give to him.

Suddenly, he turned the music off.

I said, "Hey," in protest. It's jarring when you're getting into a song and singing along and everything and someone turns it off without warning.

He said, "We need to talk."

"We do?" I said, starting to feel anxious.

He pulled over, put his truck in park. Oh! Is this where he pulls a ring out of his pocket?

He said, "I don't know how to say this... Listen, Star, you're a great girl and I've really enjoyed our time together. I mean it, it's been amazing and you're amazing. But---"

"But?" I said, my heart pounding now.

"But it's just that. We're young, you know? And I'll be leaving for college in a couple of weeks anyway and everything. So, I think..."

"So you think what? Are you breaking up with me right now? Seriously?"

"Um, yeah. I just think it's for the best. I'm sorry."

I had to leave. I just had to get away. I opened the door of his truck and got out. I walked down the street quickly, reeling, barely even noticing the cold.

As I turned onto the next street towards Big Mom-Mom's house, I looked back. Kevin's truck was already gone.

Oh, the bees. The mind buzzed like crazy.

Now I just wanted to get home, sneak into Big Mom-Mom's liquor pantry, then go to sleep. That's how I'd pass the time, while I waited to wake up from this fucking nightmare.

Hopefully, I'd wake up to Kevin calling to apologize, calling to beg my forgiveness. Maybe it was just nerves, just a momentary freak-out over the huge transition that was about to happen in our lives.

Or maybe not. I didn't even see it coming. Not at all. I thought of myself, just minutes ago, singing to Kevin with great emotion and giving him those sexy, private squeezes. While he was no doubt mentally rehearsing what he'd say to get rid of me. Planning to discard me, dispose of me, disparage me. *Disparagement. Diss. Pair. Rage. Mental.*

I went into the house and tried to hurry straight to my bedroom, after seeing that Big Mom-Mom was stationed at the kitchen table, today of all days.

"Star, come here, please," she said. *Dammit.*

When I stepped into the room, I saw that her priest, old Father Callahan, was there. I remembered him from when Bonnie Sue and Big Mom-Mom used to drag me to mass with them.

My Zozobra dolls were spread out on the table. There were a couple dozen of them. I'd had space for them in my bags and couldn't bear to throw them away at the time, after all the hours Olivia and I had put into making them. But what in the world was all this?

Big Mom-Mom said, "Have a seat, please." She sounded serious.

I sat down, wishing I could just go to sleep.

She said, "Explain, please?" waving her hand above the useless souvenirs.

I didn't really feel like talking, so I didn't.

Father Callahan broke the silence, "It's nice to see you again, Star. Your grandmother wasn't feeling well, so I stopped in to check on her. And she mentioned that she'd found these, er, things in your bedroom closet yesterday, when she went in there to collect some clothes to donate."

Ah, okay. There were some clothes in my closet that weren't mine. At least Big Mom-Mom hadn't been flat-out snooping through my stuff. I said, "Do you want me to donate them? You can have them. I don't need them anymore."

Father Callahan and Big Mom-Mom exchanged a look. Big Mom-Mom said, "Well, I'm glad you don't need them anymore. But, honey, why did you have them in the first place, and why so many of them? I've invited you to come to mass with me several times and you've always said no. But you said yes to... whatever you call this, this voodoo?"

Father Callahan chimed in. "I'm also relieved to hear that this seems to be in your past now. Sometimes young people are drawn to the more, er, exotic practices. But I must warn you, it's truly dangerous, Star. Very dark."

"You thought these were *voodoo dolls*? Oh my god... I mean, oh my gosh. They're just Zozobra dolls, souvenirs. My friend and I made them to sell at the Zozobra festival in Santa Fe. But then she... was hospitalized and we didn't get the chance to."

I sat back, waiting for them to realize their hilarious mistake.

But their expressions didn't change.

Big Mom-Mom said, "Well, it still sounds pagan to me. It sounds like a cult. Those...souvenirs... look pretty darn satanic to me. And you see? You girls were playing around with this stuff and then, next thing you know, your friend had to be hospitalized."

For fuck's sake. Okay, I'd just semi-agree with her. Whatever. "Oh. Well, I don't want them anymore, so..."

Father Callahan said, "All right, then. If it's okay with you ladies, I'll take the... Zozobra dolls for disposal, and we can consider the matter resolved, then?"

"Sure," I said, thinking about what a waste it was that now I didn't even have anybody to tell this loony story to. I could tell Brynn but I felt like she wouldn't really get it. She wouldn't howl with laughter about it, like Kevin would.

"Thank you, Father," Big Mom-Mom said. She picked the dolls up one by one with her salad tongs and placed them in an empty Walmart bag.

Big Mom-Mom said, "Now, let me get those Christmas cookies. I'm sorry they're storebought this year. I haven't felt well enough to do my usual holiday baking. Coffee, Father? And a Coke for you, Star?"

I said, "I'll get everything." I got up to do it but Big Mom-Mom made me sit back down.

Father Callahan said, "I heard you're out for Christmas break now. How did your finals go?"

I don't know what got into me. I opened my mouth to say my finals went fine and what came out instead was, "My boyfriend broke up with me. And I love him!" I put my face in my hands and sobbed.

"Oh, I'm so sorry to hear that, sweet pea," Big Mom-Mom said. She came over and hugged me. After a while, I pulled myself together, somewhat.

"I'm sorry, dear," Father Callahan said.

After a while, I calmed down enough that we could get back to our drinks and our Christmas themed sugar cookies.

Father Callahan said, "If you're up for a word of advice from an old Father…"

"Okay," I said because it would seem rude to say no.

Big Mom-Mom beamed. She really wanted me to go to church with her. I wasn't going to but it was okay with me if it made her happy to think that I might.

He said, "As you've probably noticed, we Catholics often have a different perspective on things than what's common in today's society."

I nodded. They sure did. I heard they did exorcisms, for example.

"We don't advocate dating, for very young people, for one thing. You are fifteen years old, I believe?"

"Almost sixteen. And I'm studying for my GED, so I might be out of high school soon."

"I see. You don't see yourself ready to find a husband and settle down, maybe raise children, at this time, though, I presume?"

Hell, yes. That would be perfect I thought. "No," I said.

"All right, then. I know you've been very hurt by this boy breaking up with you. If you get married at the average age for it nowadays, say twenty-five or so, that's ten years from now, a whole decade. Most dating relationships, especially among very young people, do end in break-ups, and often with broken hearts, too. It typically happens over and over and over again. What we see, we priests who do the premarital counseling, is, to be frank with you, Star, a lot of trauma in those individuals."

"Huh. I never thought of that." I hadn't ever thought of it like that.

"Yes. And that's one reason we advise that it's better to focus on other things when you're young. School, work, hobbies. Friendships. I can tell you that, in my experience, the young people with lighter dating histories do seem generally happier. They don't have all that baggage, disappointment and bitterness, to carry around. Just something to think about, my dear."

I was starting to see why Big Mom-Mom liked Father Callahan so much. He just seemed so decent. Caring. Wise. All of that. "Father" was a good name for him. I probably wouldn't take his advice, or at least not completely. But he had a point. It was worth keeping in mind, at least.

Finally, Father Callahan left. When Big Mom-Mom went to the restroom, I was able to get back to my plan of sneaking a guzzle of whiskey and just going to bed. It had been a horrendous day, being dumped by Kevin, without any notice, even. I really needed to get out of this world for a while.

#

The day after Kevin broke up with me, I didn't want to get out of bed at all, so I didn't. Big Mom-Mom was feeling a little better, well enough to go to the church basement, where they were working on holiday help for the poor, last minute gift wrapping and sorting out the non-perishables for Christmas dinner deliveries.

"Are you sure you'll be okay here alone, sweet pea? Sure you don't want to come along?"

I said, "No thanks. I don't feel up to anything today. Are you sure *you'll* be okay?" More and more lately, it seemed like I did that kind of motherly talk to Big Mom-Mom as much as she did it to me.

"Oh, sure. It will be good to get out of the house. And I'm sure the gals won't let me do much today but sit around and gab anyway."

I said, "Oh, can you take these? Maybe somebody can use them. This one is aftershave, this one is mixed nuts and this one is a wallet."

She made a sad face, knowing I'd bought and wrapped the gifts for Kevin.

I said, "Yeah, I know. Better to get them out of my face, though."

"Don't you want to give them to your dad?"

I made a funny face, then she made a funny face back. Then she left with Kevin's gifts. I went to the kitchen for a couple of gulps of whiskey straight from the bottle, then went back to sleep.

I woke to my phone ringing. Big Mom-Mom was in the hospital. She'd had a heart attack.

#

Every day, someone took me to the hospital to see Big Mom-Mom, either one of her church pals or Father Callahan. I dragged myself through getting showered and dressed, basic housekeeping and meal preparation. I limited my alcohol to one drink per night. As it was, a couple of Big Mom-Mom's booze bottles were mostly water now, since I filled them up to cover for what I'd drank. I let my GED stuff slide. It was too hard to concentrate. I was finished anyway now and just going through it all again to review.

One of Big Mom-Mom's friends even took me to the hospital on Christmas day. I made it quick, since I knew the lady's family was home waiting for her. Big Mom-Mom seemed better and said she'd probably get to come home in a few more days.

I got home at around four o'clock, my customary time to greet Thelma. I'd seen my dad, out there for some reason, early this morning, so I knew they were back from their Florida vacation. I wondered why they came home early. I hoped it was because they got into a fight or got the flu or something.

Maybe they'd even got held up at gunpoint, you never knew. I looked out the back window and there was Thelma, sitting at their patio set, all bundled up in her coat, waiting for me.

I stepped outside, stood at attention and gave her the one-finger salute. She was too lazy to even stand up while flipping me off back. I turned and shook my ass at her as a Christmas bonus.

That cheered me up a little. Back inside, I put a mug of hot water in the microwave. Some hot tea would be good on such a cold day.

Later, I sat down to eat, feeling low that this was my Christmas dinner, a bowl of canned chicken noodle soup, eaten alone. I thought of Big Mom-Mom, having an even worse Christmas than this.

The front door opened. "Merry Chrees-mas!" my dad said.

He handed me a box of chocolates. He probably just now bought them at the convenience store, sneaking around so Thelma wouldn't find out. I was suddenly furious. I remembered how Bonnie Sue would say, "This just ain't right, Frank," talking about Ree. I guess she finally figured out that he was no better.

How dare he look at me with that stupidly happy face. It was like his whole attitude was a scam that I was supposed to just play along with. I'd heard somewhere that you could sue a negligent parent for back child support when you turned eighteen. Maybe I'd do that.

I said, "Look at this," and led him to my bedroom, where the red furniture from his house had replaced the furniture that had been in there (it was now in the garage).

He looked. Of course, he must have known I took it anyway.

He said, "No do that again. Don't come eento my house."

I said, "Guess what?"

He said, "What?"

I smiled. "Your mom had a heart attack. She's in the hospital."

His face fell. "Mama? What hospital?"

"Find out yourself. If it's not too much trouble. If your wife says you can. I hope she doesn't die before you get around to it. She could be dead right now."

He looked sad. He said, "Okay, okay. I go now."

I said, "Merry Christmas, pussy."

He looked sad again, then quietly left. I cracked up laughing, pretty proud of myself. But then my mean joy turned back to sadness again. When I wasn't mad at my parents, I kind of felt the same about both of them, which was just that there was something wrong with them, something lacking in both of them that a good parent should have. I dumped out my cold soup and grabbed a bottle from the booze pantry. I took a swig but it was almost pure water.

I was about to cry but then I decided to be tougher than that. I decided to be tough as fucking nails. I turned on a cheesy Christmas movie. I ate the whole box of chocolates.

#

I didn't go back to school. I'd be able to take the GED exam in six more weeks anyway and Big Mom-Mom needed me. The hospital social worker had called me in for a discussion before the doctor would release Big Mom-Mom. I didn't know if they could really not let somebody leave, though. Maybe she could have left anyway if she'd wanted to. But after having had a couple of really good days in the hospital, she seemed weaker than ever.

I asked Father Callahan if he could drive me there and also attend the meeting with me. Big Mom-Mom trusted him and they'd probably listen to him a lot more than they would listen to me anyway.

When we went into the social worker's office, my dad was already there. I didn't know they called him, too. I hadn't really thought about it. I gave him a hug, as a sort-of apology for what I'd said to him on Christmas. I thought that was good enough, all things considered. The social worker started talking about having Big Mom-Mom admitted to a rehab center.

I said, "Rehab. You think she's on drugs or something? I hardly ever even see her drink alcohol."

The social worker, who said to just call her Diane, said no, this was a different kind of rehab center. It was for people who didn't need to be in the hospital any longer but weren't yet well enough to care for themselves at home. Big Mom-Mom would have round the clock nursing care at the rehab center.

"You mean a nursing home? Oh no. She's not going to a nursing home. I'll take care of her." It seemed only fair to me. She took care of me when I needed it, so I should return the favor.

That led to a whole big discussion about my age and my GED plans and everything. In the end, it was decided that my dad would sign Big Mom-Mom out of the hospital and officially take responsibility for her. And then he could handle any further arrangements from there.

I think it was just a way for the hospital to stay out of trouble. They probably didn't want to get involved with a fifteen-year-old dropping out of school or with approving a fifteen-year-old to be anybody's full-time caretaker.

It also put a stop to any thoughts I'd had about possibly dropping the GED thing and just finishing high school. I probably wouldn't have anyway but now it was a solid no.

From what the social worker said, Big Mom-Mom was really ill and she might not be getting that much better. In other words, she might not even be around to see me through two and a half more years of high school.

Big Mom-Mom wouldn't be home for a day or two longer. The doctor still had to sign her out. On the ride home, I told Father what I'd said to my dad on Christmas. I could really see Father doing confessions. Even though he was old and such an authority figure, there was just something about him that made you want to blab your problems to him. I felt like he wouldn't be horrified or shame me, even if he was super religious.

He said, "And now you feel bad about what you said, correct?"

"Yes. I mean, to be honest, even though I used a crude word and it was Christmas, what I said is true and I think he deserved it. But I still wish I wouldn't have said it. The hurt look on his face hurt me. Well, at first I laughed about it. I guess it felt good to just unload the anger I have for him. I mean, I had to spend Christmas alone. But I felt bad after that."

He said, "I understand. Of course you're angry and disappointed. But as far as feeling bad about your reaction, I'd say that's your conscience talking to you. It's up to you to maintain a high standard for yourself at all times, even if anyone around you does not maintain that same high standard for themselves. Do you agree?"

I said, "Yes. I agree."

We were in front of Big Mom-Mom's house now. Father walked me in, and told me to call if I needed anything. He said that between himself and the parishioners, there was always somebody available to help.

He said, "One more thing. Your grandmother wanted me to tell you, she plans to have a meeting here when she gets home. It will be the three of us, plus an attorney."

"Why?" my heart seized up. "Is she sending me away?"

"Oh no. Nothing like that. In fact, the opposite of that. She wanted me to tell you ahead of time to prevent the kind of worry I just caused. I'm sorry."

"That's okay. But what is the meeting about?"

"Apologies for being blunt here, but she's worried about what will happen to you if anything happens to her. She wants to be sure you could continue to live here and continue with your studies."

"Oh. Will my dad be there?"

"No, Star. He won't. And your grandmother asks that you not mention it to him. All right?"

"Ah, I get it. She doesn't trust Thelma."

He didn't answer directly but he kind of smiled and kind of nodded. He said, "Your grandmother wanted me to tell you this right away, to take at least some of the worry off your mind. All right, then. Take care, my dear." He turned to go.

"Thank you, Father," I called after him.

#

Big Mom-Mom had been home from the hospital for three months now. We fell into a routine, which I'd have liked, if it hadn't been because Big Mom-Mom was so scarily weak and frail.

It was like one person went into the hospital and a different person came out of it. I brought all her meals to her on a tray and even had to help her take a bath and get dressed every morning. I especially dreaded going to check on her first thing each day. I was always afraid that she might have died in the night.

But there was nothing to do but just get on with it. I'd get Big Mom-Mom presentable and the daily chores done in the morning. Most days, we'd have visitors in the afternoon or evening. Big Mom-Mom had endless church friends who seemed to have organized themselves into a rotating visitation schedule. They were nice ladies, mostly, a lot like Bonnie Sue and Big Mom-Mom.

The church ladies brought over a lot of homemade food, too. My dad stepped up also, or at least it was stepping up for him. He came by four or five evenings per week now, though he still never stayed more than a few minutes each time.

I'd review my GED stuff at night, after everybody left. Until I finally got to take the exam, that is. It was such a relief to finally get it over with. I knew at the time that I did well. But I still had to wait for the official results in the mail, before I could start the interior design program I had picked out. I'd found an online course. It was perfect, since I needed to stay home and take care of Big Mom-Mom.

Brynn and her mom, Miss Annette, were supposed to be here soon. I had Big Mom-Mom settled in with her pillows and blanket on the sofa, where she liked to lie during the day and watch her shows. She'd just asked me to fetch her beauty bag, which contained things like her brush and hair clips, lipstick and that awful White Shoulders perfume that always made me sneeze. It was a good sign though, that she was feeling well enough to want to pretty herself up.

Company always improved her mood. And today was extra special because Miss Annette was bringing her mother along, a widow named Esmerelda, who was about the same age as Big Mom-Mom and who we hadn't met yet.

Miss Annette was also treating us all to takeout pizza and, best of all, two nail techs who did house calls were coming over to do everyone's nails.

Big Mom-Mom said, "I don't even want to think about what that blooming bill will be, two techs, a house call and five sets of nails? Mercy."

I said, "Well, maybe not a whole lot more than the bill you paid for four of us that time?

That was at the salon at least, instead of a house call. But remember, then we also had pizza at the restaurant, which always ends up costing more than takeout."

"Eh, I'm old and can afford it." She checked her lipstick in the mirror. I'd never thought about how much money Big Mom-Mom had before. The attorney hadn't said any dollar amounts to me either, when he and Father came over a few weeks back.

The attorney had just said something about how my dad's debt to Big Mom-Mom would be forgiven, whatever that meant. I didn't pay much attention because he'd been talking to Big Mom-Mom, not me. Everything else would go to me.

I said, "What kind of nails are you getting? I think I'm gonna go for the medium length acrylics this time, painted black."

"Black? Oh my."

I said, "I know, it does sound pretty Halloween-ish, doesn't it? But I saw it online and I thought it looked really stylish. Which surprised me."

Our visitors pulled up in the driveway. I went out to greet them, since I had to get the mail anyway.

"Hi!" Brynn said, getting out of the driver's seat.

"Hey. Wait... Did you drive over here?"

"Yes! Just got my license last week. I can help you get yours, if you want."

"Wow, thanks." I definitely wanted that drivers license. I felt a jab of envy that Brynn got hers first. Brynn wasn't supposed to do anything before I did.

I greeted Miss Annette and Miss Esmerelda, then waved them into the house. I said, "Big Mom-Mom can't wait to see you all. I'll be right in."

I walked to the end of the driveway and there in the mailbox was the envelope that would contain my GED exam results. I felt like I was holding the ticket to my real life.

I opened the envelope and peeked and of course I'd passed all four subjects. Now I was officially done with high school.

When I announced that I now had my GED, everyone made a big fuss over me.

All through the pizza eating and nail stuff, Big Mom-Mom talked about the party she was going to have for me, to celebrate what she called my graduation. Her guest list included Miss Annette, Brynn and Esmerelda, who she'd seemed to bond with immediately. Also, Father and my dad and Big Mom-Mom's ten thousand gal pals from church.

It was a lovely afternoon. I hadn't seen Big Mom-Mom so lively in a while. She recited all her plans for my GED party again to my dad, when he stopped by that evening.

I never did get my GED party, though. The next morning when I went to check on Big Mom-Mom, she was dead.

#

She looked peaceful, like she'd just slipped away in her sleep, so that part was good, at least. I didn't know what to do, though. Calling 9-1-1 didn't seem right. How could it be an emergency if someone was already dead? It didn't seem like the police, fire or ambulance non-emergency numbers were right, either, since there hadn't been a crime or a fire and it was too late for an ambulance. I could call a funeral home but I didn't know which one. Then I thought to call Father and wondered why I didn't think of it in the first place. He'd know what to do.

He came right over and suggested I just go get ready to start my day while he handled everything else. When I came back into the living room, showered and dressed, the house was already swarming with church ladies. One of them swooped me into a hug and others lined up behind her. It was too much. The ladies were very kind (except for the tall one with the New York accent, who was bossy). But they'd been Big Mom-Mom's friends, not mine. I didn't feel up to dealing with them.

I excused myself and went to my bedroom, locking the door behind me. I wished everybody would go home.

I curled up under my covers and just let the sadness wash me over. A while later, I heard my dad and Father in the hallway, outside the bedrooms.

My dad said, "No, thees ees my mother's house and I take thee valuables. For safekeeping."

Father said, "First of all, I'm sorry for your loss, Francisco."

"Thank you," my dad said.

Francisco? Oh, right, that was my dad's full first name. And Father would have known my dad when he was a child.

I heard Thelma. She said, "Uh-uh. Oh no, you don't. Frank, this is *your* mother's house and *you* are the one in charge here."

Father said, "No, ma'am. I am, in fact, the one who is legally in charge here. Now, I must ask you again to put that jewelry box back on the dresser and leave the bedroom immediately. This isn't seemly."

"Oh-ho-ho, I don't think so. Come on, Frank. Let's see what's in the closet."

Father said, "That's enough, now. You two need to put that back and leave right now or I'll have to call the police."

"Thee police?" My dad sounded surprised.

"Yes. This house and everything in it was left to Star, and it's under my care until she is of age. None of it belongs to you. You may direct any questions to Mateo Santiago. He's the attorney involved in carrying out your mother's wishes."

My dad mumbled something, then I heard Thelma's squawking fade away, as she followed my dad out. I hoped Big Mom-Mom's body had already been removed from the bedroom, at least, before Thelma tried to take her jewelry.

It was like my dad barely even existed. Like he was an invisible air current or something, just drifting around until he was pushed in any direction. I wondered what would make a person like that. I had no idea. I guess I just didn't know him very well.

I drifted off to sleep and dreamed about heaven. I mean, if there even was a heaven. It was soft and fresh and pretty, with colorful songbirds.

#

Brynn and I were ready for it, the first day the subdivision pool opened. Her house was the first place I drove to after I got my license. I stopped by to pick her up.

It seemed right, since she and her mom helped me practice driving and took me to get my license.

The pool gates opened and only a couple of other people were waiting, so we settled in on a pair of nice loungers. We came prepared, with towels, sunscreen, sunglasses, new pedicures, bottled water and novels.

It was a Saturday morning. We had the whole sunny day stretched out in front of us.

I said, "So, do you have any plans for the summer?"

She said, "Oh, I didn't tell you. I got a job at the hospital. It's only part-time but it's permanent, not just for the summer."

"That's great. So much better than wasting your time in fast food or something, you know? What will you be doing at the hospital?" When Brynn found out I had started my course to becoming an interior designer, we started talking about what she wanted to do. She decided, with my help, I think, that she wanted to be a nurse. The pay was pretty good, the job outlook was good, it was meaningful work *and* there were related jobs you could do on the way, rather than needing a four year degree to even get started. She wasn't sure she wanted to do college straight through. In the nursing field, she could become a nurse's aide or an LPN first, if she wanted.

She said, "I'm just a patient transporter. But they said that's just the official job title. There's other stuff involved, too."

"Well, great. Hey, it's definitely a foot in the door, right? I'm sure you'll learn a bunch of stuff that will help you later, from working in a hospital."

"Yeah." She said, sounding more sure about it now.

"Oh, I'm starting a new thing, too. I mean, aside from my online design course. Mine is also part-time. I'll be an assistant to an interior designer. I'll just do, basically, whatever she needs me to do."

"Nice! Oh, did you know Kevin's back home for the summer?"

I felt a little dizzy, suddenly. Getting dumped was just so humiliating. First, I hoped and hoped he'd change his mind. Now I hoped I'd never have to see him again. "Oh, really?" I said, trying to be uninterested. I took a sip of water, then rifled around in my beach bag for my book. The Kevin topic made me anxious.

Brynn said, "You'll never guess who he's dating."

Somebody better than me. Prettier, cooler, you name it. I said, "Have you read this book?" I really doubted she had because I'd grabbed it off Big Mom-Mom's bookshelf that morning on my way out the door and it looked pretty old. I was trying to change the subject.

"Nope, I don't recognize that book. Anyway… Do you want to know who Kevin is dating? I couldn't believe it."

Brynn wasn't that good at picking up on hints. I kinda did want to know who it was, though, in spite of that part of me that actually likes myself. I gave in. I said, "Who?"

"Selena."

"Selena? What? You're kidding, right?"

"Nope." Maria José saw them at the mall, holding hands and everything.

I said, "Hmm. I wouldn't have expected that." It figured the chisme came from Maria José. I shouldn't have worried, though. I didn't really feel anything about it, one way or the other. It seemed like all of them, Kevin, Selena and Maria José and even Brynn, sort of, were from a different lifetime.

I thought of what Father had said, though, about all the drama and trauma caused by getting into relationships when you're very young. I kinda hoped Selena wasn't taking it seriously, because I couldn't see Kevin being serious about Selena. She was kind of silly and everything but she didn't deserve to have her heart broken.

#

Talk about a small world. The interior designer I was to assist was Ms. Hernandez. When I first read her name, I hadn't even considered that she might be the mother of chisme queen Maria José Hernandez.

As it turned out, Ms. Hernandez was gossipy, too. But unlike Maria José, Ms. Hernandez was hysterical. Her imitations of clients, suppliers and anyone else who pissed her off, just slayed me.

This one rich man we were doing a living room makeover for got on Ms. Hernandez's nerves because he kept changing his mind on things we'd already ordered. After the third coffee table change, Ms. Hernandez pulled her ears out to mock how his ears stuck out, and exaggerated his way of over-emphasizing each syllable. She flounced around her office, mimicking him about coffee table shapes until I was rolling.

I wondered, though, if Ms. Hernandez's finely tuned sense of appearances was the real reason Maria José got that parrot beak-ectomy. I could see the former lack of proper proportion on Maria José 's face driving Ms. Hernandez bonkers.

We were finally done with Mr. Ears, as Ms. Hernandez privately called the man who kept changing his mind. Next week, we were to start decorating an indoor pool area. I'd never seen an indoor pool in somebody's house before. I couldn't wait.

I was in a good mood on the drive home. Things were starting to come together again. Painful feelings would still hit me a couple of times a day, mostly over Big Mom-Mom passing and Ree not wanting me in her life. But then I'd remember that thing I'd heard from Devon, of all people, about how dwelling on pain from the past was being ungrateful for what you had today. That thought helped me every single day.

It was after five when I got home but I thought I'd take a peek and see if Thelma was outside, anyway. I'd stopped stepping out on the back patio for a while after Big Mom-Mom died. I was just too sad to bother with it. But then I started thinking about the bitch trying to take Big Mom-Mom's jewelry, and I got back into the ritual. I also asked Father to have someone come out and change the locks on Big Mom-Mom's house, or I guess now I should say on my house.

Aha. There she was. Sitting at their patio set with a drink. I could only hope it was anti-freeze. It was a beautiful evening, though. The sky was periwinkle-tinted, and splashed with gold and orange above the mountains in the distance.

When Thelma saw me on Big Mom-Mom's patio, standing at attention as per protocol, she leaped right up. It seemed like she was happy to see me. That made me happy, in an angry, fucked up way. I nodded. She nodded. Our middle fingers were extended. Then we both turned sharply and in unison, and went back into our respective homes.

I'd come home tired but the flipping-off ceremony energized me. I still had some studying to do for my online decorating class. I made two peanut butter sandwiches real quick and sat down to eat in front of the TV. I'd take this short dinner break, then do my online lesson.

I wondered what Father would say about my ritual with Thelma and cracked up a little to myself, thinking about the way one of his eyebrows would lift up when you said something questionable. Man, I bet he'd heard some dirt.

I thought it was on the television at first, when I heard it. *Ruh-ray-ooo, yip, yip. Yip, yip, ruh-ray-ooo.*

Ree! Oh my god, it was Ree.

I dashed to the front door and yanked it open. But Ree wasn't there. I walked out onto the front porch and down the driveway and looked all around. No Ree. *What the hell?*

That's when I saw it. It was dusk but not dark yet, so I don't know how I missed it. Something was on the front porch, next to the door. I stepped closer, thinking I must be somehow mistaken about what I saw.

But I wasn't mistaken. It was an infant carrier, a car seat, whatever you'd call it. It held a tiny baby. A baby with pale skin and light, reddish hair.

I rushed around to the side of the house, still searching for Ree.

I came back and sat on the porch. It had to have been Ree. Surely, she'd be back soon.

Waiting for Ree to come back summed up a lot of my life, come to think of it. I sat there until it was completely dark out and the baby started to whimper.

I picked up the baby in the carrier and brought it into the house. What else could I do?

The baby needed a diaper change. I grabbed a clean dish towel and used that, with masking tape to secure it on both sides.

Soon, he cried again. He worked himself up into a red-faced frenzy. I remembered babysitting for Lella, with her five kids, back in Albuquerque. I'd have to buy some formula and a bottle. I'd had to leave his little outfit off because it was soaked. I got another clean towel, this one a bathroom face towel, and tucked it in around him, in his carrier. I strapped him into the backseat of the car and drove to the store.

A half hour later, we were back home and he was fed. I put him on a clean blanket, on the couch next to me and tried to think of what to do next. I felt like Ree was asking for my help, loud and clear, by leaving her baby with me. If she even knew I was here. She may have just thought she was leaving him with Big Mom-Mom. Either way, I'd just have to take care of him for now and hope she came back soon.

I'd only bought the one can of ready-made formula and a bottle because all I could think about at the time was getting the baby fed so he'd stop crying. But Ree still wasn't back. The baby would also need diapers, wipes, clothes, pacifiers, baby blankets and more formula. I should go get it all before the stores closed for the night. I put him back in his carrier and drove back to the store.

#

Three days later, I was exhausted and Ree hadn't come back. The baby only slept for two or three hours at a time. He cried a lot. Then, he stopped crying completely. He seemed too still. He felt hot. He was sick. I had to do something right away. I called Father.

Father drove us to the hospital. I sat in the backseat, next to the baby.

In the end, I didn't have a choice and neither did Father. Apparently, you couldn't just bring a newborn into a hospital and refuse to give them any information. And, of course, Father was a priest so he wouldn't try to fudge his way through the intake questions, anyway.

I went into the exam room with the baby. But after the doctor finished treating him, a nurse came in with a security guard and they took the baby away.

Father and I were told to follow the social worker to her office, so we did. Another security guard escorted us, which was embarrassing. But I guess they didn't trust anybody, not even a priest, when you showed up at a hospital with a newborn that wasn't yours and a crazy story. The social worker was the one named Diane, the same one who we'd met with before Big Mom-Mom came home.

Father told me, "It's okay. You're doing great, dear. Just answer her questions the best you can." I was glad to have him there reassuring me because I felt like a total rat, the world's worst narc, even though at the same time I knew that I'd had to get the sick newborn to the hospital and that none of this craziness was my doing. Yet here I was, at the center of another big mess, as usual.

Diane said, "You're saying this baby was left on your doorstep?"

I nodded, miserably.

"All right then. And you think you know whose baby it is, but no one actually told you that?"

I nodded again. I felt like she didn't believe me. I felt like she might think it was really my baby.

"Okay, then. We can't know for sure that somebody didn't, say, take this baby from his mother without permission. Maybe for revenge, even. Or because they didn't want to share responsibility for him."

I started to tell her that I heard Ree's coyote call. But I knew there was no way she would think that was enough. Besides, it sounded insane.

She said, "I know you don't want to get anybody in trouble but do *you* think it's reasonable for someone to leave a newborn baby on a doorstep? What if you hadn't been home, or... Well, hon, it's simply not adequate. It's not safe. See?"

I had to admit, she had a point.

I also had to admit that the thought of being stuck with a baby made me want to crawl into a deep, dark hole and never come out anyway.

But my feelings seemed wrong to me. Well, at least this way, it wasn't my fault. I *couldn't* take the baby with me now, even if I begged to.

Diane said, "All right. Now, I hope you'll leave here proud of yourself because you made the right call. You did the right thing and the intelligent thing. Let's not forget that a sick newborn can even die, if they don't get timely medical care. One more thing. Before you go, I'd like to get a swab from your mouth, to help us identify this precious angel for sure. And I'd like your permission to contact you again, if we need to ask you any more questions. Would that be all right?"

I nodded yes. A nurse came in and swabbed the inside of my mouth, then Father drove me home. He offered to have one of the church ladies come stay with me but I just wanted to be alone.

I was a wreck for the rest of the night and most of the next day. I mean, regardless of how it all came about and other details, I probably just gave my own brother away. That goddamn Ree.

#

I met Ms. Hernandez at her office on Monday, as we'd agreed on. I'd have to work extra hard this week. Besides three days coming up with Ms. Hernandez, I had to make up the online coursework I missed over the weekend, when Ree's baby was here.

Ms. Hernandez and I were to ride together to the house with the indoor pool, in Ms. Hernandez's BMW. Big Mom-Mom's old PT Cruiser was far too old and ratty. Ms. Hernandez said appearances were extremely important for interior designers. You had an image to project. You didn't pull up in front of a client's home in anything that wasn't late model and expensive.

She said, "How was your weekend?"

I nearly burst into tears. But I just said, "Fine. How was yours?" Ms. Hernandez was not someone you should give too much personal information to.

As if to prove me right, she immediately went into a hilarious acting out of her goody-two-shoes daughter (Maria José) and the weekend theatrics brought about because Maria José's crush liked somebody else. It was soon revealed that Maria José had been talking about Kevin and Selena.

Ms. Hernandez's comical imitations cracked me up, at first. But underneath the hilarity of her flailing and shrieking "I can't live without him!" it was kind of mean and disloyal.

Also, I'd never thought of it before but I could actually see Kevin with Maria José. Maybe not for a couple more years because Maria José seemed pretty high-schoolish, for lack of a better word. But she and Kevin were both kind of serious and studious. Selena was a wild child party girl who took all the easy classes.

"Well, here we are!" Ms. Hernandez chirped, pulling up in front of the house. I was disappointed. I was expecting a mansion. It wasn't a dump or anything but it was only a typical older, one-story house in a regular 1980's subdivision. It probably had, like, three bedrooms and two bathrooms.

The two-car garage seemed to have been converted into living space. There were tall, narrow windows where the garage doors would have been.

I said, "They turned the garage into an indoor pool area?"

She nodded. I followed her to the door, carrying the big case that held her computer, tape measure, paint color cards and stuff.

An older woman let us in and showed us the pool area. It all looked brand new but the woman said it had come with the house and they'd recently had the pool re-surfaced and the walls primed.

We moved to her dining room table and I set up Ms. Hernandez's computer. Ms. Hernandez told me at the office that she'd start by showing the woman examples of a few different styles that were common for indoor pool areas, and also discussing how to integrate it with the décor in the rest of the house. She said you'd want to try to get hired to do additional rooms in a house.

The woman, who introduced herself as Jeanette, said, "Can I interest you ladies in a coffee or a soda? I have diet Coke and regular 7-Up. Oh, and this is my son, Michael. He'll be weighing in, too. He's decided to stay here for college instead of going away, so the pool room will be mainly used by him and his friends. For the next few years, anyway."

I said I'd have a Coke, if it wasn't too much trouble. Ms. Hernandez had said that a client offering you a drink or snack was like an offer of friendship, in a way. Accepting their hospitality helped built rapport.

Jeanette went to get the drinks and I felt Michael's gaze on me. I peeked over at him now and then during the discussion, which I was supposed to listen to but not participate in.

I liked Michael a whole lot, so far. That is, as much as you could like someone you'd just met, without being a kook. I liked his dark eyes and dark hair, which were the opposite of Devon and Kevin's blonde-ishness. I liked his thick build, too. He wasn't tall and slim like Devon and Kevin. I also really liked that his name didn't rhyme with Devon and Kevin.

Well, that part was kind of ruined when I discovered that his last name was Evans. But it was okay. He gave me a shy or sly smile and I forgot Father's advice about staying away from boys.

After work, I saw Thelma sitting out at her patio table, waiting for me. I wondered if Michael and I would ever stand out there and flip Thelma off as a couple. I wondered if he'd ever bring his swimming pool friends along to flip Thelma off, too.

The End

If you enjoyed this book, a review at your point of purchase would be most appreciated.